RATNA TRANSLATION SERIES

THE ROCK THAT WAS NOT

AND OTHER STORIES

GITHANJALI

TRANSLATED FROM TELUGU BY
K. SUNEETHA RANI

RATNA BOOKS

Original Telugu copyright © Githanjali

First Published in English Translation 2019
English Translation copyright © K. Suneetha Rani 2019

ISBN   978-93-5290-738-0 (POD)

Published by RATNA BOOKS
An imprint of Ratna Sagar P. Ltd.
Virat Bhavan, Mukherjee Nagar Commercial Complex
Delhi 110009, India
www.ratnabooks.in

GITHANJALI is the pen name of Dr Bharathi, MS, who by profession is a Doctor, Sexologist and Psychotherapist. Based in Hyderabad and a member of the Revolutionary Writers Association, Telangana State, Githanjali started writing in Telugu around the age of 13 and won the Sri Sri Memorial Award for poetry. Since 1990, she has been writing with a clear Marxist perspective. Her novel, *Aame Adavini Jayinchindi* (She Conquered the Forest), was published in 1998 and won the Appajosyula-Vishnubhotla Award. Since then, she has stopped taking awards from private and government literary organizations. Her second novel, concerning caste and gender – *Pada Mudralu* (Foot Impressions) – is still unpublished.

Her first collection of stories in Telugu is *Bachedaani* (The Uterus) depicting individual and collective problems of women, including reproductive rights, sexual and health issues, sexual and domestic violence. Her second book, *Pehechaan* (Identity), which has been translated into Hindi, is a collection of 16 stories concerning issues of Muslim women, such as child marriage and trafficking, teenage pregnancies and polygamy. Her third anthology, *Palamuru Valasa Bathuku Chithralu* (Stories of Migrant Lives from Palamuru), has stories of sufferings and struggles of people who migrated from Palamuru to Kashmir. Her forthcoming novels focus on rape, manual scavenging and Hindu fascism.

Dr K. SUNEETHA RANI is Professor at the Centre for Women's Studies, University of Hyderabad, Hyderabad. Her areas of interest include Gender Studies, Cultural Studies, New Literatures in English, Comparative Studies and Translation Studies. She has extensively published research articles in English and translations in English and Telugu. Her latest books are *Influence of English on Indian Women Writers: Voices from the Regional Languages* (edited) published by Sage-Stree and *Identities and Assertions: Dalit Women's Narratives* published by Primus Books.

The complex woman–man relationship demands mutual care and compassion, but is often sickened by the patriarchal mindset compelling women to live as mere sexualized and commodified bodies. In the twelve stories in this book, Githanjali explores day-to-day issues in a woman's life, which are generally not talked about or for which society has only a male perspective. The stories depict how women are labelled, isolated and stigmatized; how they are often made to suffer the trauma of being treated as breasts, a vagina, a womb, and a 'boxing bag'. Like a deft surgeon, Githanjali identifies and separates the malignancies corroding the sociocultural fabric. For their path-breaking themes, these are the stories of resistance, protest and transformation.

Eleven of the twelve stories in this collection are taken from Githanjali's latest book of short stories in Telugu, titled *Husband Stitch: Strila Laingika Vishada Gadhalu* (Husband Stitch: Tragic Stories of Women's Sexuality).

Contents

one

§

The Rock That Was Not

S TARS WERE TWINKLING IN THE DARK SKY, the sea roaring
below. Perhaps the day was afraid of humans – it became
night. Moonlight consoled the sulking night and spread itself
to lighten the darkness. The cold breeze was blowing hard.
The sandy beach gave out the heady, salty scent of the sea. I
stood on the seashore, stretched out my hands and raised my
head to see the stars in the sky. I was engulfed by the bliss of
tranquillity and the fabulous beauty of the dark night.

Suddenly, the sky burst into two and the stars began to
fall in heaps. Some fell on the earth. Some exploded midway
in the air. Ear-shattering sounds. I closed my ears with my
palms. The broken stars were falling on the sea and the beach,
turning into stones. Those were perhaps the quartz stones
mentioned in the counselling session. The explosions and
downpour ended. Silence again. I was covered up to the neck
in that downpour of stones. With difficulty, I cleared the

stones from around me. Just as I was getting out, white sand began falling from those stones.

Slowly, the white sand turned into thick liquid and flowed towards me. It got into me through my feet, reached my chest and filled my breasts. It was not only in front, but also on my back that a pair of breasts, filled with sand, popped up. Gradually my head disappeared. A headless trunk with four breasts, I dragged my legs buried in that liquid on the seashore. That midnight, I was searching for my head and plunging my arms in the vacuum.

My breasts are full, bigger… Am I a statue of rock now?

From somewhere, the sound of laughter spread in waves. A male voice, my husband's husky voice whispered into my ears, 'You're so sexy, Prathima.' Two hands appeared in the sky and came towards me. I tried to run away from those hands, but was unable to move my feet. My breasts, filled with the liquid from the rocks, were moving heavily. Those hands grabbed me and squeezed my breasts. Excruciating pain. No, there was rock liquid inside; the breasts would burst. I felt suffocated and cried, 'No,' pushing the hands away. I tried hard, but I was not strong enough to push away those hairy, strong male hands. Those hands did not stop. They continued to squeeze my breasts harder and harder. Then came a big sound like a balloon bursting and both the breasts had burst. The rock liquid, mixed with blood, was flowing down my body. Unable to bear the pain, I tried to wipe it and screamed, 'Amma…'

Prathima woke up startled. Her whole body was sweating.

Was that a dream? She was astonished. She put her hands on her chest and heaved a sigh of relief. Her hands felt her breasts. They were secure. Her breasts – no, no, her husband's breasts…her husband had got them made.

She looked at her husband. He was sleeping cosily, snoring.

Prathima could not sleep after that. The dream haunted her. She had had this dream several times. It kept coming back to her. Whenever she had this dream, fear spread down her spine. Was her identity merely her breasts sprouting from her headless trunk? That too four breasts! At least her dreams should have her identity; or, maybe her identity was her struggle, the running away or the bursting of her breasts.

Exactly six years ago, those breasts had become a part of her body. It was ten years since she had got married. Her husband, Ashok, was tempted by the dowry that her father had offered and had married her. She was thin and lean. On the nuptial night, Ashok felt her breasts and said with impatience, 'Empty…nothing there. I don't feel any desire even when I touch you. Che, how did your mother give birth to you? You're like a pole.'

She knew that her nuptial night was going to be like that. She spent those three nights in silence, shedding tears. One cheap comment or the other and sniggers at her breasts every day. It was the same in her college. She was called 'chapatti'. Why didn't she have a fully developed body like other girls? That question always plagued her. Looking at the 'developed' girls, she started rejecting her own body. Her mother took her to many doctors. Ayurveda, homoeopathy, naturopathy, herbal therapy, diet, yoga – she tried everything. Nothing worked. Her mother used to overstuff her with food. Worried about her marriage, her mother became a shadow of herself. Ashok became acquainted with her father in the course of his business dealings. Her father noticed Ashok's greed for money and used that to get him married to her.

Ashok used to taunt her, 'I married you; no one else would have.' His eyes invariably hovered on women's breasts at weddings and other functions. He drank up the housemaid, Chandramma, with his eyes.

In Prathima's presence, Ashok would watch 'full' bodies on the internet and behave nastily. To counter her look of disgust, he would insult her with no shame, saying, 'What should I do? You don't have it, do you?' She compensated for this agony by joining a college as a lecturer, though she did not need money. She kept herself busy without a minute of leisure. She never wore the synthetic and silk saris that she liked the most. She wore only cotton saris to look full.

She remained silent when her mother enquired, 'Is he looking after you well?' The gynaecologist tried to convince her, saying, 'When you give birth to children, there would be hormonal changes in your body. Don't worry.' But she did not have children even after three years of marriage.

'You won't have children!' and 'Where are the feminine qualities in you?' were Ashok's barbs. Perhaps by feminine qualities, he meant that women should be passive and docile and have full breasts.

All kinds of tests were done. None of them showed any defect. But they did not have children. They rarely had sex. During sex, he would make obscene comments about her body, talk about women with huge breasts, like Nagma, Rambha and Rasi, and sigh in despair. She hated such psychological prostitution. There could be a defect in her body, but she had respect for herself. Whenever she refused him, he mocked her, 'You have nothing, yet you are arrogant.'

One day, he made her sit in front of the computer and spoke to her in a loving tone, 'Look Prathima, come here, I'll show you something.' It was about silicon implantation – it was a boon for women like her. He showed her pictures of heroines who rose to the top position after silicon implants. She did not understand what top position she had to rise to. 'Look, our problems will be resolved. If my dissatisfaction increases and I go to sluts, both of us will get terrible venereal diseases such as AIDS. Just think about it.' The initial tone of pleading evaporated. The more she rejected his suggestion of silicon implants, the more threatening he became.

Filling the rock liquid in her body? Her heart had already turned to stone. Should she get artificial breasts prepared for a husband who did not want the love in her heart, a husband who treated her breasts as mere lumps of flesh? Just to satisfy her husband and to keep her family together? Without shame, he spoke to her parents. They also started nagging her. 'He may already be going around with other women. Please agree to what he says, Prathima dear,' said her mother in tears.

She had to oblige. It was hard to keep in her body

something that was not hers – the rock liquid made from stones. Would she be a human being in flesh and blood then? She would become a rock. She died of shame when the assistant plastic surgeon took the measurements of her chest. Before her marriage, when she used to go to the tailor to get her blouse stitched, the tailor would take the measurements with a sarcastic smile on his face. He would say, 'I know your measurements – 26-28, isn't it? I'll stitch the blouse, you can go.' Somehow, she had endured that humiliation. Unable to control herself, she had once told her mother about it, weeping. Mother had gone to the shop and slapped the tailor left and right. After that, she always accompanied Prathima to a lady tailor.

The counselling before the surgery was in the form of a patient education session. She was surprised to see the women who had come for the surgery. All of them had dark circles around their eyes. They were there to alter their chest, which was like a flat ground. At the session, they were all getting ready for the change to take place in their bodies, listening to everything that was being said, without any expression. 'This silicon liquid is made of either quartz rock or white sand.' They showed them pictures of heaps of white sand and rocks. Would those rocks decide our future! The counsellor continued: 'You won't feel your husband's touch on your nipples and breasts because the nerve-edges would be damaged. You should be prepared for all this.'

Husband's touch and the feelings it gave rise to! When did her husband's touch create feelings and responses in her?

He compared her body and her incompleteness with other women's full bodies and insulted her with lust, dissatisfaction and irritation.

'Lumps could form; sometimes the liquid could leak. One breast could appear like two if it is not arranged with care. They could lose shape. If firmly squeezed, the silicon pouch might break and blood might clot. Cancer cannot be detected in a mammogram.' She couldn't hear any longer. She stepped out. Should she bear all that? On the one hand, they warned her that there was a possibility of such things happening; on the other hand, they said that you could satisfy your husband completely and regain your bonding.

'As for me, I'm ready to bear anything. My husband's satisfaction is important to me. Wretched money doesn't really matter,' said Niharika from Banjara Hills.

'I had to sell my gold. My husband refused to give money. He doesn't want to borrow. My parents didn't have money,' said the middle-class Soujanya from Alakapuri, with tears in her eyes.

'What should I do? He always calls me a pole. He goes around with other women. Already, I've contracted diseases from him. Recent reports show that I have herpes. I'm going through hell with these wounds, burning and pain. What will happen to my children if I get AIDS? That's why I wanted to go in for this operation,' said Revathi, as if in a daze.

It wasn't just her. Many women, like her, were being sacrificed to their husbands' carnal desires and uncultured behaviour, and were mortgaging their bodies and health to prevent their families from disintegrating. Her situation was the same.

One night, when Ashok was in a good mood, she pleaded with tears, 'I don't want this. I'm scared. Joint pains, loss of hair, blood clots in the breasts, the pouch leaking and bursting, cancer! I can't bear the thought of all these happening to me.' He had fulfilled his desire by then and was fondling her body. His hands loosened at once. 'You don't have breasts at all. Why would you get cancer? Why do you think everything will happen to you? Che, your thinking is always negative. You never think of satisfying your husband. Can't you do this much for me? I knew you had such a big drawback, yet I married you.' His face turned miserable in a second.

He quickly added, holding her chin, 'For my sake, please, nothing will happen. It's a very simple operation.' He pulled her close to him and started to fondle her again.

It was like the butcher stroking the goat to prepare it for the sacrifice, saying, 'Get sacrificed now for the people who will eat you up dotingly.'

The surgery was done. The weight of a thousand tons of stones on her chest, pushing her into an abyss.

Her husband looked at her proudly, like a sculptor ogling at the large breasts he had sculpted, though there was no need to.

She did not feel his touch before she had the rocky breasts and continued not to even after she had them. All the feeling was for her husband's benefit. Great satisfaction. Now he was goading her to accompany him to parties and functions.

Earlier, he used to say to her face, 'I feel ashamed to introduce you as my wife.' Now he wanted to take her along as an exhibit. How could she bear this?

Within a month, there was clotting of blood at the stitches in the right breast. She experienced hellish pain. Blood was drawn out with a syringe. Her husband enquired from his plastic surgeon friend, 'Nothing would happen to the silicon pouch inside, would it?'

It did not matter what happened to her. Why was she going through this? She never wanted them. Her joints started aching and her hair began to fall. He pretended not to hear and notice, though she told him about everything. If she said, 'I'll get them removed. I'm unable to stand and teach in class,' he would say, 'Who asked you to work. Stop it. You have a maid at home, don't you?' She had no right over her body. The rocky liquid pouches artificially sprouting from her body ridiculed her, troubled her and created an unbearable hell for her. She had dreams about trying to pluck them out with long nails, rocky fluid mixed with blood spilling from her nipples and drowning her...

It did not feel like she was cleaning her body, but was cleaning the stones which did not merge with her blood and muscles, and which were not hers. She was reminded of the counsellor's words, 'These will be placed in the body only after laboratory tests to check if they match the tissues in the human body.' Didn't he say that? Not body, they did not match her heart. Her heart was refusing, weeping and trying to get rid of them. Sometimes her husband squeezed the breasts passionately. She was frightened, thinking what if they broke inside, as the counsellor had said. If they burst, he would get them fitted once again. She would try to stop him. He would get incensed, saying, 'Why, what happened? You wouldn't know pain and touch, would you?' What happiness did her husband, who had no concern for her, derive from an unresponsive body? In any case, all that he wanted was the body. He did not expect any response. Sometimes thoughts like how she would feed the children troubled her. Would she have milk with the silicon implanted in her body? She forgot to ask the surgeon.

If there was this problem with her husband, there was another problem with the people around. It was humiliating to see them staring at her body – quite unlike the way it used to be in the past – and whispering to each other and laughing under their breath. She started to cover herself completely with the pallu of her sari when she went out. She joined another college, unable to bear the nasty looks and laughter of her male students and colleagues. She was amused when she saw her parents feeling happy about their daughter's secure family.

One day, she began getting a stabbing pain in her left breast. It continued to trouble her every day from then on. She told her husband about it one night. Squeezing her breasts hard, he said, 'Are you acting to escape?'

She had a series of dreams. In her dreams, she was making an effort to pluck out the rocky liquid pouches and feeling the pain of it. She woke up with that pain. It was not natural.

She knew something was happening to her. Her husband said, 'Perhaps something has happened to the pouches. We shall go to the doctor tomorrow.' His worry was not about something happening to her, but about the possibility that he would be deprived of pleasure if something happened to the pouches.

Her husband's face showed relief when after examining her, the doctor said, 'Don't worry, Ashok. Nothing has happened to the silicon implants.' She felt like laughing at herself. When she asked the doctor why she had that pain if everything was all right, the surgeon said, 'Madam, you should see the gynaecologist. I suspect there's some growth inside.'

Her heart missed a beat. 'It is not clear because of the implants. It would be better if you got a mammogram done. Tell the technician that you have implants,' said the gynaecologist.

She went to the laboratory the following day.

'Stand up, remove the blouse, place both of them on that wooden plank and move closer,' the technician instructed.

'But for me...' she stuttered.

'What is this? You have to cooperate,' the technician scolded her.

'I have silicon implants.' She almost died of shame saying that.

'Oh, is it?' the technician gazed at her breasts in amazement.

Wretched tester machine. Each breast had to be held, placed on the wooden plank and moved close to the machine,

11

another wooden plank squeezed it firmly from above. Pain and fear as if the breasts were going to split. Pain when reminded of her experience with her husband. Pursing her lips and holding her tears back, she endured that tester.

At last she said, 'Why all this? I will get the implants removed.'

'No need. How much I struggled! How much I spent!' His voice was stern. She had no right over her body. This body belonged to him; that's all! He had hidden silicon pouches in her body like gold in a bank locker. She should remove them from her body for her comfort. She should take a decision about her body. She could not bear the pouches filled with the rocky fluid, which did not belong to her. Something was happening inside her. She could feel it.

The gynaecologist said, 'It is not clear in the report. The report is normal. No tumour. I'll prescribe medicines. Take them; the pain will subside.'

'Didn't I say there won't be anything? You were worried for no reason,' Ashok scolded her.

She took the medicines. But there was no improvement. The pain increased. One day, she fainted and was admitted to the hospital. When she regained consciousness, her mother was sitting beside her and weeping. She couldn't understand. She slipped into unconsciousness again.

When she gained complete consciousness, she heard her mother's choked voice, 'She was complaining of pain for the past six months. We got this X-ray done. My daughter has got some pouches in her breasts, to look beautiful. She did that because my son-in-law put pressure on her.'

The doctor examined her and her face became grim. She suggested blood tests and an MRI scan. Perhaps the doctor could not understand even after the examination. She should request the doctor to remove those stones that had become a burden to her. The gynaecologist who had seen her reports earlier had looked very young and inexperienced. She should have suggested these tests.

Prathima shut her eyes feebly. When the pain became intolerable, they gave her painkillers and sedatives. The pain subsided a little by the next day. She was alone in the room. She took a magazine lying next to her and started reading.

'Nani, do you know what a secure place this is? I find the peace that cannot be found anywhere else in the world. Do you know how comfortable I feel here? Did you ever sleep here at all? Oh, you must have slept on your mother's bosom. But you were a child then. Would you remember that touch, pleasure, warmth, security and aroma of your mother's sweet milk? What do you know about the power of this bosom? I will always be thankful to you and to your two breasts that give me this happiness, intoxicating pleasure and security every day. Don't ask me to move away from here. This is my permanent address. Do not shift my head away from your heart. I will be frightened. I will become aloof. I will start sobbing. You have become my mother again by allowing me to sleep on your bosom. You turned me into a suckling infant. Even if you move away for a moment, I will cry like a lonely child deprived of the mother's lap. Have mercy. Hug me closer to your bosom. Let me listen to your heartbeat that chants my name. Do not distance me from the lullaby that your heart sings for me. Do not throw me into this cruel world.'

The story went on like that. Tears welled up in her eyes without her knowledge. A husband, with his head on his wife's bosom, was speaking in tears. This society had men like Ashok who looked at women's breasts as mere sex symbols and lumps of flesh that satisfy their lust. In such a society, this man was addressing breasts as bosom, a sacred place that provided him rest and security, and was pleading with her not to distance him from there. Her husband got the artificial pouches fixed in her body like trophies on a wall because she did not have those lumps of flesh. Did he ever hear her heartbeat and the agony behind it?

Even now, his face showed anxiety about something happening to his property and the fear that something might happen to the rocky liquid pouches. She wished he would say, 'Nothing will happen to you, I am there. We will get those wretched pouches removed. You are important for me.' He wouldn't say that. He would never say that.

In any case, the decision this time was hers. She wouldn't carry that burden any longer. She was not a rock. The MRI report came. They were all sitting in the doctor's chamber – she, her mother, her father and Ashok. The doctor's face was serious – some pain and some hesitation were visible.

'Sorry, the MRI scan shows a tumour in the left breast. There are other changes too. Traces of cancer are seen in the blood test. You should be ready for anything. A small sample of the tumour has to be sent for a biopsy.'

The doctor kept giving details. Mother burst into tears. Father looked frightened, with tears in his eyes. Ashok's face was expressionless. He suppressed his irritation with difficulty. At first, she couldn't understand anything. Slowly she could. The doctor meant there were chances of her having cancer. 'The implants on the left side might have to be removed for the biopsy,' the doctor said. What good news! 'Please remove it, doctor; remove that wretched thing.' She got angry.

'Prathima, wait,' said Ashok. His concern and care were for the silicon pouches and not for the tumour under them. Those pouches would be removed at least for the biopsy. She wanted to tell them to remove both the pouches. The doctor looked at her strangely and laughed when she asked, 'Doctor, is there no tumour in the other breast?'

'Why, do you want it in the second breast as well? Do you think cancer is like a cold? There is no problem in the right breast. But don't worry. It may not be cancer. We can't detect cancer till the advanced stage due to these silicon implants. But why did you want these?' said the doctor angrily.

It was a blow for her. She pointed at Ashok and almost yelled, 'Not me doctor, my husband got them fixed for his pleasure.'

'You see the consequence, don't you? You should have accepted her as she was. Now, she is in danger. You are safe. Why did you play with her life?' the doctor rebuked Ashok.

She gestured to stop Ashok, who was about to say

something. 'I'll get the biopsy done tomorrow. The report should come after a week,' said the doctor and left.

She was alone at home. The silicon pouch on the left breast was removed for biopsy. That place was empty. It was looking awkwardly wrinkled. It looked as if it was coiling with anger for Ashok having played with her.

Disgust and anger were writ large on Ashok's face. He kept silent. He did not touch her even once. She had turned again into a dry stick and a pole, as far as Ashok was concerned.

She was very tense. What if the report revealed cancer? She was overwhelmed with fear and grief. Would she have to die? Her life was not ideal, fulfilling and happy. But she had hope. She wanted to do well as a lecturer and wanted to become a professor. She still remembered her happiness when she had got the best lecturer award. Her aim was to become a professor. She struggled hard to complete her PhD. She should live at least till she got that degree. She wanted to live as she was the only child of her parents. They did not have a son. Who would look after them if she died? She should not get cancer. In fact, she should have protested vigorously. She should not have allowed them to fix the rocky liquid pouches in her body. Before the pouches were installed, the counsellor had said that cancer cannot be detected by mammography with the silicon pouches in the breasts. How much she had wept, fearing something like that would happen to her! How much Ashok had scolded her! He had blamed her for always thinking negatively. Now, she was going to die. No, he had murdered her. He would live. He would marry a woman with a good figure. He would harass that woman's parents for property. God, please save me from cancer. She decided to get the implant removed from the right breast as well.

Once again, they were all sitting in front of the doctor with the report. There was another doctor as well. The gynaecologist introduced him, saying, 'This is Dr Veeresam, the cancer specialist.' Fear was lurking on their faces. She could hear her own heartbeat. The cancer specialist said, 'Sorry, the cancer is in the third stage. It is spreading from the left breast to other parts of the body. That tumour should be surgically removed immediately. Then you must undergo chemotherapy.' She almost collapsed when the gynaecologist said, 'Sorry, you should be psychologically prepared. You should be bold. Get admitted to the hospital.'

Mother wept uncontrollably; father held her close. Mother cursed Ashok, 'You wretched fellow, you destroyed my daughter's life.' Ashok had been avoiding all three of them for the past few days.

Chemotherapy was started. She began shedding hair. She became weak and thin – like her husband said, a dry stick. The silicon pouch was protruding from the dry stick-like body. It was looking ugly. Che, she must get it removed. Wish this one had also got cancer. Should it be removed only if it had cancer? Even before she took the decision to get it removed, cancer had attacked her. Death was close. She must get it removed from her body before she died. She should live without it until she was dead. Her body should be burnt without it being inside her. She liked her natural pole-like body. She took an appointment with the plastic surgeon.

Prathima sat facing the doctor in the hospital. She explained her condition to the plastic surgeon.

'Ayyo, I'm sorry. We had warned you at that time. You took the decision.' The doctor was sad. She said smiling feebly, 'It is printed on cigarette packets and whisky bottles that consuming these things is dangerous and might lead to cancer. This business is similar, doctor.'

The doctor's face went pale. He stuttered, 'But I told Ashok that you should get an MRI done after two years to detect abnormalities, if any. Didn't he get that done? I'm sorry.'

She looked at him, shocked. 'He did not tell me. It's his selfishness. At least you should have informed me, the patient. It was your duty. I would have got it done. I wouldn't have fallen prey to cancer now.' There was anger and sorrow in her voice. 'In any case, now I want this silicon implant to be removed from the right breast. I don't want it. I can't bear it. This is my last wish. Please, I don't want this,' the doctor was surprised at her harsh tone.

'After consulting Ashok...' said the doctor. Ashok was his friend.

'No, who is he to decide? I'm not his property. He is responsible for my condition. He is a murderer. You cannot ask him,' she snatched the mobile phone from his hands, pressed the lock button and threw it onto the sofa. She was trembling with anger.

'I'll get admitted tomorrow. You have to remove it. My

mother will sign as my guardian.' The doctor remained quiet as she spoke with resolve.

> (*Dedicated with tears to M.N.,*
> *whose cancer was not detected due to silicon implants,*
> *and who struggled to live but was embraced by death*)

§

two

Offering

M ALANBI WAS SITTING ON THE COT beside the jasmine vine in the courtyard. Just then, Tabassum, her twelve-year-old eldest daughter, started sweeping the place. She sprinkled water on the ground and put broken rice for the hens. Before that, she had been washing the vessels and cleaning the front of the house. There was no flour in the kitchen to make rotis. After Malanbi had become bedridden, all the housework had fallen on the child's shoulders. Her mother-in-law was there, but she would not budge from where she sat.

Tabassum had to stop going to school to slog at home. She told her mother, 'Forget it Ammi, don't think too much about it.' She toiled from morning till night. She got her two younger sisters ready, fed them whatever there was at home and sent them to school. If there was nothing at home, she went to the nearby shop, bought buns, gave them to her sisters with tea before sending them to school. She cooked for everyone. She even kept water in the toilet for her Dadiamma (paternal grandmother). She cleaned without any disgust the spitting pan that her grandmother dirtied after chewing paan. Added to that, Malan's sister-in-law and her children and husband visited them often. Tabassum had to take care of them as well. She worked without taking a break, never cribbing.

Malanbi wanted to help her daughter. She herself was not well, but hated to see her daughter toil like that. Tabassum was kept away from school and play. She worked like a thirty-year-old. Malanbi wiped her tears. Her stomach started paining again. She was told that her uterus had to be removed if she had to be cured of the bleeding and pain in her stomach. But she had to give birth to one *mard bachcha* (male child). How would it be possible if the uterus was removed? How did it matter to the doctor?

Tabassum came in and asked her, 'Ammi, what vegetables should I cut for curry?' Malanbi made an effort to get up and go to the bathroom. She said, 'Give me brinjals and knife, I will cut them.' Blood streamed down her legs like water from a tap. Malanbi felt dizzy and collapsed, calling out, 'Tabbu.' Tabassum cried, 'Dadiamma, Ammi has fainted. Please come fast.'

Malanbi regained consciousness in the hospital. The doctor shouted at her so much that she lost her senses again. 'How many times have I told you to get the TV X-ray done? There is a big tumour in the uterus. You'll die,' she scolded

Malan and her husband, Afsar. The doctor had been telling Malan for the past two years to get the CT scan done. Malan avoided it fearing that the scan might reveal something dreadful. Her neighbour, Suseelamma, also had excessive bleeding. She had gone for the TV X-ray (CT scan). Her uterus was removed as there was a big tumour in it. Her husband apparently started torturing her a lot. He started going to another woman, saying that he could not have sex with a woman without a uterus. How much Suseela had cried when she shared all this with Malan!

She didn't know what mood Afsar was in. He told her to go for the TV X-ray.

The TV X-ray was done. Blood and urine tests were also done. As feared, a big tumour was confirmed in the uterus. The doctor sent a sample of it for biopsy. The reports showed that it was a malignant tumour that could turn into cancer in the future. The bleeding would also increase. The doctor said that the uterus had to be removed, or else she would bleed throughout the month, which was risky for her life. The blood test report revealed that she was severely anaemic. The doctor prescribed injections to increase the level of haemoglobin in Malanbi's body, saying that she would be transfused blood before the operation, if necessary. Malanbi blabbered like mad, saying no, no. She cried, 'Ya Allah, I won't get the uterus removed. Let it be, let me die, let whatever happen...' Her husband fell silent.

MALANBI HAD GONE TO Jahangir Dargah, beyond

Shamshabad, to make her offerings. She fed the fakirs and the banjaras with mutton biryani, seeking a *mard bachcha* and to keep the *sautan* (rival wife) at bay. But she gave birth to a girl child the third time as well. All's Allah's wish! What could one say! Both her mother-in-law and husband had attacked her. Her mother-in-law had grumbled and her husband had bashed her, saying, 'Shameless woman, you can't give birth to a *mard bachcha!*'

Once, when she was beaten with a staff, her head was injured and needed ten stitches. Her parents and children cried a lot. At least this time she should give birth to a *mard bachcha* and silence them. But how? What did she have to do to give birth to a *mard bachcha*? As she worried over this, the disease affected her. Her mother-in-law started goading her, 'It's not in your fate to give birth to a *mard bachcha*. Oye woman, my son will marry again without making a noise. You should just agree.' She grumbled in front of the children, 'Everyday you are bleeding, my son has no pleasure with you. Where did we find you at all?' Malanbi died of shame when she heard those words.

Women bore either twins after twins or had miscarriages and operations, or else got tumours in the uterus, like her. They had to carry either children or tumours. They had to either suffer their husbands or shed blood throughout the month. Cursed be this woman's life. Malanbi felt suffocated, as if her mother-in-law and husband were sapping all her energy. Her three children were sleeping nearby. She looked at them again and again, saying, 'My daughters,' and crumbled inside. What if something happened to her? What was it to her husband? He would get another woman even before her dead body was removed. Who knows how much the *sautan* would torture her children! 'God, save me please,' Malanbi prayed through her tears.

She waited as if she were waiting for the moon in the month of Ramzan for her husband to lovingly say, '*Mard bachcha* is not more important than your life. Get the operation done. I won't marry again.' Malanbi's grief surged up. Along with that surged up the pain in her stomach. Fearing that her children might wake up hearing her sob, she went into the courtyard.

She sat on the granite stone under the jasmine vine and kept weeping. She was frightened to see the darkness around her, but gathered courage when she saw the stars in the sky. After a while she went in, bolted the door and lay down. The children and mother-in-law slept in the front room. Meanwhile, Afsar had probably come; there was a bang on the door with a stick. She opened the door. Afsar was drunk. Malan asked, 'Shall I serve food?' He fell on the mat, muttering something she took to be 'No'. Malan too went and slept in her place.

In the middle of the night, Afsar was coiling around her like a snake. She pleaded with him, saying, 'No, it hurts. I'm still bleeding. No, leave me alone, I fall at your feet.'

'You bitch, you can't give pleasure, and you don't allow me to go to others either.' He inflicted blows on her, forcibly separated her legs, pulled the blood-soaked cloth and flung it to a corner and overpowered her. Malan stuffed a cloth in her mouth, fearing that her children might wake up if she screamed with pain and that she would be shamed.

Afsar got up panting and looked at the blood spreading on the bed sheet. 'Che, what kind of life do you have.' He spat on her and went into the bathroom. Tears streamed down Malanbi's eyes and blood from between her legs. She got up with difficulty, holding the walls and doors, collected the blood-soaked bed sheet and the blood-soaked cloth that her husband had flung away, and went towards the bathroom. Afsar came out. He spat on the floor once again, looking at her, and went to the bed. It was not the first time. If she did not agree, he threatened to go to another woman. Malanbi collapsed, agonizing in the bathroom. She felt as if she was going to die of pain.

'REMOVE THE TUMOUR from the uterus, Doctoramma, keep the uterus,' Malanbi cried and gestured with her hands to say no. The doctor said, 'You're asking me to keep the uterus and remove the tumour. You're telling me what to do! Don't talk for a while.' She called Afsar to her consultation room. Malanbi was being given blood. Because of what Afsar had done, Malanbi had bled the entire night. The following morning, her people had taken her to the government hospital when she had fainted.

The doctor scowled at Afsar, who stood in front of her, 'Didn't I tell you not to force her? Her condition is critical. She was already bleeding, still you did it like a beast. On the one hand, you say you want to marry again and on the other hand, you ask her to give birth to a *mard bachcha* and you rape her. A police case can be registered against you, do you know that?'

Afsar stood with folded hands, red eyes and head bent.

He said in a low voice, 'Do the operation, Doctoramma,' and left the place. He walked towards Malanbi's ward, cursing her with swear words, why should she tell the doctor about last night!

Malanbi lay like a corpse. On the bed beside her's was a woman called Sujatha. Her husband had left her there and gone away as she was giving birth to a girl child. She was crying along with her three girls. The doctor on duty was trying to console Sujatha. 'Ask your husband to meet me sometime tomorrow. I'll explain to him that it is not in the hands of the woman, it's the man who is responsible for the birth of a girl child.'

Afsar heard that conversation and wondered if that doctor was mad. Those words soothed Malanbi. But when she looked at Afsar rushing towards her in anger, she knew those soothing words were wasted on him.

The doctor had night duty that day. She sat in her room thinking about Malanbi's refusal to get operated. Why did she say no? Why did she take such a risk when she had three children to look after? She wanted the tumour to be removed but the uterus to be retained, as if the uterus was a treasure trove of precious stones and as if her life would end if it were separated from her body. In fact, her life would end if it remained in her body. How should she explain this to Malan? She had already lost a lot of blood. If she became more anaemic, she wouldn't even be fit for the operation. Why was she suffering so much? Why was she going through such mental agitation? She knew Malanbi's husband was a demon. But, was there any other reason? What if she counselled and convinced Malanbi about the operation?

The doctor came to the special ward where Malanbi was. Tabassum slept hugging her mother. It looked like Malanbi was lost in thoughts. It was a shared room. On the bed beside Malanbi was Sujatha, with the four-day-old infant in her lap, sitting and staring like a mad person. Her two small children and her mother were sleeping on the floor.

The doctor said, 'Sujatha, get some sleep. It's too late into the night.' Sujatha wiped her tears. The doctor said, 'Don't cry, I'll speak to your husband. Sleep now.' Sujatha put her baby to sleep on the bed and she too slept.

Malanbi got up with a jolt when she heard the doctor's voice, 'Salaam Doctoramma, haven't you slept yet?' she asked, her face was looking pale. The loss of blood had made her complexion go white.

The doctor sat on the stool beside Malanbi's bed, explained to her why she was there and said, 'Now, you have to talk, Malan.' Malanbi first laughed, then she wept for some time. The doctor did not stop her and let her weep. She kept holding Malanbi's hands.

'What shall I say, Doctoramma? What is there that you don't know? You delivered my children; don't you know my distress? My husband brought another woman even when I was healthy. You know about that. It was you I had come to when I consumed poison. It's you who saved my life. You remember, don't you? Somehow I threatened her and sent her away and brought him back on track.

'Now, what else would he want if my uterus is removed? My husband is waiting for an opportunity to bring another woman once you remove my uterus. Wouldn't it give him a clear excuse? That's why, remove the tumour but do not remove my uterus. After the tumour is removed, I'll take treatment from you to be able to have a *mard bachcha*. I'll give birth to a *mard bachcha*, and I'll give my husband an answer as a slap. Give me good tablets and injections to increase the blood in my body. I'll eat lots of greens. But please don't remove my uterus. I fall at your feet, I entreat you with folded hands,' Malanbi started to cry again. The doctor's head was reeling. Malanbi said what she had anticipated. Malanbi was struggling to somehow protect her uterus. Was she trying to save her uterus or her life?

Tabassum woke up at the sound of her mother's sobs, pressed her mother's head to her bosom and consoled her, asking her not to cry, as if she were used to doing that. Tears welled up in the doctor's eyes, but she controlled herself and said, 'Look Malanbi, you won't conceive in this condition. And even if you do, the foetus won't survive. Listen to me. I will convince your husband and mother-in-law. Don't worry but think about your children. It will be very dangerous if you lose blood like this. The tumour in your uterus will turn cancerous.' The doctor continued to speak for a long time. Malanbi kept listening. The following morning, Malanbi went home. She prayed that if she was saved this time, she would go to Jahangir Dargah once again to make offerings.

Malanbi went in and out of the hospital for saline and blood transfusions five or six times. Whenever she went, the doctors and nurses on duty started to write in the case history, 'Bleeding, fibroid uterus, advised hysterectomy, patient not willing to undergo surgery,' without even examining her. Malanbi's husband beat her more often and did not promise that he would not marry again. Malanbi pleaded with him with tears in her eyes, 'I fall at your feet, please swear on the children that you won't marry again after my operation.' Afsar did not promise. He kicked her and abused her, 'How are you concerned about it? Get the operation done.'

Afsar did not listen to the doctor's repeated words that 'Malan will agree to get operated if you promise.' The mother-in-law started shouting, 'How you are torturing my son! You'll go to hell,' as if Malanbi was in heaven. Her parents also pleaded with her, but failed to convince her. All of them became quiet. Although Malanbi was gasping for breath due to excessive bleeding, she did not get admitted to the hospital, nor did Afsar promise her.

With the excessive bleeding and fainting, Malanbi looked like a corpse. This became a routine for people around her. If her parents took her to the hospital for examination, the nurses there would comment, 'The one who sheds and takes blood. The A-group woman has come.' They infused glucose and blood whenever she was admitted to the hospital. They tried to convince her, saying, 'Get the operation done.' She said, 'I will, I will,' gasping for breath and waiting for her husband to come and say, 'I won't marry again, you get the operation done.'

One day, Malanbi was admitted to the hospital. Her pulse was slow and her blood pressure fell. She slipped into shock.

Blood was being infused. Saying, 'Don't operate, don't do it,' and pulling the oxygen mask off in that unconscious state, Malanbi passed away never to shuttle again between home and the hospital, with her uterus safe and secure in her own body.

three

§

OCN

'Hymakka, Arunakka is dead...' Latha's voice on the phone.

'How, why?' Hyma was flabbergasted.

'Six o'clock last evening, she poured kerosene on herself. Come to the Gandhi mortuary, fast,' Latha disconnected the phone. Did she pour kerosene? Did that mean suicide? Hyma's heart was filled with grief. What and who had killed Arunakka? Was it the psychological pressure that had piled up on her over the years? Pressure...pressure on an enthusiastic and vibrant activist? Was it apathy? Akka flowed like a song, fusing her life with people's problems and singing to resolve them. How did she become silent? Why did Akka die?

'The seasoning is burnt,' Chakravarti shouted, coughing. He was sitting relaxed in the front room and reading a newspaper. Hyma rushed into the kitchen. The seasoning was burnt. Hyma turned the stove off and opened the windows completely for the smoke to go out. Couldn't he have gone into the kitchen to check when she was on the phone? Che, what kind of a person is he! He won't change.

Chakravarti came into the kitchen with the newspaper in his hand and enquired, 'What happened? Whose phone?'

'Didn't I tell you to mind the seasoning?' Hyma could not control her anger. She continued in a choking voice, 'Arunakka has died, it seems.' Chakravarti was shocked, 'What happened? It was only the other day that she sang on the occasion of the International Women's Day at the Press Club.' He was shocked again when Hyma told him the reason.

Hyma put the chapati dough in the fridge and told Chakravarti as she got ready, 'I've made rice and dal. You make an omelette and pack the children's lunch boxes. Give the children a bath, feed them and send them to school. I'm going to the Gandhi Hospital mortuary.'

'I'll pack rice and dal in the lunch boxes, okay?' Chakravarti said wearily.

'Why, don't you know how to make an omelette?' Hyma said even more wearily.

'When should I come then?' asked Chakravarti.

'I'll phone and tell you,' said Hyma and stepped out in a hurry.

THERE WERE MANY activists in front of the Gandhi mortuary – leaders of people's organizations, akkas and annas. They were all looking depressed, with disconsolate faces. Since the previous day, they had been shuttling between the hospital and the mortuary and consoling Arunakka's husband, Hanumantharao, who was the state president of the Raitu Coolie Sangham. Hyma went and stood near him. Hanumantharao greeted her with a listless look. His palms were burnt and had blisters.

What should she say? How should she console him? Should she ask him why and how it happened? Did he have an answer? No, not just him; no one – except the blazing hearts of women – had answers to the why, what and how of matters related to women, their sufferings, hardships, tears, murders and suicides... Should one search for the reason for Arunakka's suicide in the silent heart under her charred skin? Don't know. No no, Akka had agonized the other day, grieved and finally burst out. 'I'm vexed Hyma, I feel like going away somewhere, I feel like vanishing. What remains? Why all this? Despite having such knowledge and consciousness, I'm languishing in the kitchen all the time, cooking, getting boiled like vegetables and becoming effete. Why should only I cook? Every day I have to cook for ten to fifteen people. Why? I too feel like eating when someone cooks for me, without my having to go to the kitchen. I too want to eat and drink when someone lovingly offers me lunch, breakfast and tea. All the time, only I have to cook. The same rice, same dal and same curries – my hands are getting tired of cooking. What if I chopped off these hands! I don't know Hyma, these days I have crazy thoughts. If I see kerosene, I feel like immolating myself with it. I feel like cutting my nerves if I

33

see a knife. I feel like severing my hands. I feel like drowning to death if I see water. Death, death is beckoning me. What if I died once in peace instead of dying for days and months in the kitchen? Tell me, Hyma. Your Anna feels bad. "I'd have cooked if I had time, but I've no time, I'm a full-time worker," he says. I was also a full-time worker once, wasn't I? He remained a full-time worker after marriage. But I became a part-timer for the movement and full-timer for the kitchen, and remained like this. People come and go and ask for food, saying they are hungry. They are activists working for people. My conscience doesn't agree. So, I cook and feed them. But there is some pain in me, as if I have lost something. Didn't our Vimala say that kitchens should be burnt? Of course, they should be burnt down. Activists' lives are also like that. Isn't it strange? I'm going mad, Hyma. I've no enthusiasm now. I can't sing now even if someone asks me to do so. Discussions drain me out. I've a strong urge to die one of these days,' Arunakka cried with a reddened face. Tears were welling up like lava from a volcano. Disgust, anger, helplessness – Hyma was afraid that Arunakka would really burn the kitchen that very moment.

Hyma said, 'Talk to Anna...' Even before she could complete the sentence, Aruna said with angst in her eyes, 'What do I say to a person who travels across places, comes home in the middle of the night and says that he is hungry and that I should serve him food if there is any, or else it's okay? He wakes up in the morning, eats something and goes away for work again. I fought with him, saying why should I alone be taking care of the housework and cooking. He says, "Am I not a full-timer Aruna; shall I leave the work? I don't have any objection to doing housework and cooking. But the movement makes demands of me and my time. Or else should we all eat in a hotel? But we don't have that economic status, do we?" Does the movement require only his services and not mine? Why does the movement not demand my creativity and writing skills? Why this difference?'

When Aruna offered to make tea, Hyma said, 'No Akka, I just had some before coming here,' as she did not want to send Arunakka into the kitchen again. Akka smiled, 'Forget it, come, make tea for yourself and give me a cup as well.'

'Akka, don't be hasty. Don't entertain any thoughts about suicide. Remember the responsibilities on you. Let us go to the doctor. First, you shift that kerosene tin to the attic. Don't keep it in front of your eyes at all,' said Hyma.

'I travelled through the villages with much enthusiasm as if the entire world was mine. Now, when I've become a slave to this kitchen, conflict is becoming inevitable. I feel disgusted even while eating food. The feeling that the food is not for me but for others is enveloping me,' Arunakka's voice sounded pathetic. Meanwhile, there was a knock on the door. Aruna opened the door. Six activists from Warangal with suitcases and bags in their hands entered, asking, 'Is Anna at home?' They were all known to Aruna.

'Akka, we are very hungry. We'll eat and go to the meeting. It's long since we ate food cooked by you.' Their talk was familiar. Hyma couldn't dare to look at Akka's face at that moment. How was Akka's face? Hyma's eyes welled up when she was reminded of that incident. Were tears disallowed there? One had to be dignified. No, tears don't abide by any principle.

'Hymakka – Arunakka left us,' Jamuna hugged Hyma, wailing.

'How did all this happen, Jamuna?' asked Hyma. 'Don't know, Akka. Our activists came from Khammam last night for a meeting on the cotton farmers' suicide. She served them dinner, happily it seems. She too participated in their discussions. What happiness! She must have struggled within herself. The next morning, the visitors had tea and went to work. Anna was still asleep. Her son goes for tutorials in the morning. When no one was around, she went into the kitchen, poured kerosene over herself and set herself on fire. Unable to bear the flames, she ran into the drawing room howling. By the time Anna got up and saw this, she was severely burnt. Anna covered her with a blanket and put the flames out. Anna's hands also got burnt. He brought her to Gandhi Hospital with the neighbours' help. She had 90 percent burns. The doctors said it was unlikely that she would survive. As they had feared, she passed away early in the morning. She went through hell before leaving. When I asked her why she burnt herself, she said in her death statement, "I felt like doing it. I did it. Anna is a good person. He did not cause me any trouble, that's all".' Jamuna was trying to control her sobs. Meanwhile, Sarada came, with a shrivelled face, her eyes swollen with weeping. Saradakka worked in a slum.

'Somehow Arunakka had been behaving like a crazy person in the recent past. The other day we completed our work in the slum and went to Arunakka's house as it was nearby. We were all tired of singing, talking and moving around since 4 o'clock. We had had tea once in a house in the slum, that's all. We were very hungry. Sujatha is the youngest of all; she didn't know about Akka. She said, "Akka, we are hungry." That was it. Arunakka screamed in a fury, "Hunger? What hunger? Cook if you are hungry. Don't you know how to cook? Go, cook; I won't cook." Sujatha was petrified. She stopped crying with difficulty after I consoled her.' Sarada sounded distressed.

'The post-mortem will take one more hour, it seems,' Uday gave the information. They were all waiting for Arunakka. Her son, Rajesh, was sitting under the tree with a drooping face. Some party workers were sitting with him, immersed in some discussion. The stench of the charred skin had spread in the wind…the smell of a human being burning…the smell of death…flowing in waves.

Hyma did not feel like talking to anyone. Her heart was full of memories of Arunakka. One day, she had persuaded Arunakka to accompany her to a psychiatrist. When Aruna told the psychiatrist about her repeated longing to pour kerosene on herself and burn herself, and her thoughts about death, the psychiatrist had said, 'Engage in some work that you like to divert your mind. Read books, listen to music and go to places that you like,' and prescribed antidepressants and other medicines. Aruna was asked to relax. When Aruna said that she felt averse to cooking and that the kerosene tin, knife and the planked knife invited her when she went into the kitchen, the doctor said, 'Stop cooking for a few days and go on a jolly trip.'

Akka laughed, cracked up. Hyma knew why Akka was laughing. The doctor's face showed irritation, 'Why are you laughing like that? Look at me, how busy I am! I arrange everything for everyone at home and cook before I come to the clinic. Isn't it our responsibility! Going by what you said, I should also be having an aversion to cooking.' She had the air of one who had given a great example and said, 'You can go now.' How easily she dismissed Arunakka's problem! When would these people understand why Akka and women like Akka suffered from psychological issues? What an easy solution the doctor had suggested for Akka's problem! She should go on a jolly trip and divert her mind, read her favourite books and listen to music, it seems! Could women escape from cooking and housework even after doing all this? Didn't they have to return to the kitchen after the jolly trip? Should women's creativity and intelligence burn to ashes in the kitchen? Should women's wishes get buried in the kitchen? Men give different reasons to escape from housework and cooking. Who should tell these doctors that the patriarchal system controlled women? When would they understand that antidepressants were not the solution for women's psychological disorders?

On the prescription was written 'OCN'. When they asked the doctor what OCN meant, she smiled and said,

'Obsessive compulsive neurosis…obsession means getting the same thought again and again and compulsion means doing the same thing again and again. It can be cured. She needs a diversion.' Compulsion, obsessive compulsion, doing the same thing repeatedly for years…no change, no creativity…forgetting everything else about the heart …wouldn't one go mad?…Wasn't every woman being subjected to obsessive compulsions?

'I got a great disease, Hyma,' Aruna said laughing after we came out. Jolly trips, it seems. Akka travelled in villages in the hot sun, pouring rain and freezing cold, without bothering about diseases and infections… She moved around bearing menstrual pain…sang suppressing the pain. The doctor had advised her to take bed rest when she was pregnant with Rajesh. Had she paid this advice any heed? She was adamant, and travelled across villages. She had got labour pains as she was singing and delivered the child while the meeting was in progress. She had her jolly trips in slums and villages. Not only did she listen and sing but also made her songs reach people. After Rajesh's birth, everything happened so quickly that she had to stay at home to look after him and over time got confined to the kitchen. She spent years like that. That severe dissatisfaction singed Akka's heart like wild fire. Arunakka's laughter that day had intimidated Hyma.

Sankaranna – Jamuna's husband – was consoling Rajesh, who was crying thinking of his mother. Sankaranna had great theoretical knowledge, working capacity, activist spirit and leadership qualities. His speeches were very inspiring. In his lectures, he said that women should get educated and become knowledgeable, and that men should share housework, but it seems he did not do any work at home. He did not even wash his underwear, it seems. Jamuna was illiterate. Sankaranna said in meetings that women should be educated, but he didn't make the least effort to educate his wife. He was deeply dissatisfied that she was illiterate. Jamuna said, 'He speaks at length at meetings outside, but you should see him at home to know his true colours. It was said during the last Women's Day meeting that men and women should do housework and kitchen work together. Didn't they resolve that men should cook for a week after the meeting? He cooked once, that's all. It was the same again. All this is a game for them.' It seemed as if Arunakka agreed to this right there and then. How nice it would be if Arunakka would come and drive these men to the kitchen, saying, 'What are you doing here? Go and work in the house and kitchen!'

Hyma's temples were throbbing, on the verge of splitting. Arunakka was brought on the stretcher, wrapped in a white cloth like a heap of flesh. The domestic toil subjected her to obsessive compulsions, rolled her soul into bundles and suffocated her to death.

Rajesh broke down on seeing his mother, a bundle of flesh. Hanumantharao was staring at her reddened face. All of them, full of emotions, surrounded the stretcher. They offered red salutes to Arunakka, with tears and flower bouquets.

Arunakka's face looked blurred through Hyma's tears. She felt as if Arunakka's face said, 'Look Hyma, I died. Didn't I do a good thing? I wished to burn the kitchen down, but I burnt myself.'

Arunakka's body was shifted into the van and sent to the cremation ground. Akkas, annas and workers all followed her in a procession. Akka was cremated…completely. Arunakka, who shone like the sun and lit the red dawn in thousands of women… Arunakka, who pushed forward the message of the red without getting scared of the guns, had succumbed to cooking and the kitchen and got burnt.

Hyma felt drained out. Vacuum, vacuum here and there. Was it the same everywhere? Can't women escape from obsessive compulsions? Jamuna shook her by the hand, asking, 'Hymakka, where would you go? Let's go to our house.'

'No Jamuna, I've to go home. The children must be starving. I'll go, we'll meet again,' Hyma said.

Where was her journey leading to – to the obsessive compulsions? Hyma's head was splitting. Unintentionally, her feet took her home; no, towards the kitchen.

four

§

Nymphomania

'MUMMY, TAKE THESE PILLS,' Neha stood in front of me, impatience in her voice. She kept checking text messages on her mobile phone in one hand while holding medicines in the other. Her body language indicated as if she was waiting for me to take the drugs so that she could run away from there – the posture of a bird about to fly away.

'Please sit. I've to talk to you for ten minutes. I don't need these pills, please sit.' I held Neha's right hand, which held the medicines, requesting and cajoling her.

'No need, I've heard enough. The doctor and daddy told me everything. In any case, having seen everything with my eyes, what more do I have to hear? Daddy has given me the responsibility of making sure that you take the medicines. I'll leave if you take them. Take the medicines now…you know that I'm preparing for the GRE.' With disgust and anger showing on her face, the twenty-year-old Neha looked exactly like her father. I controlled my anger. I had brought up this child sacrificing my postgraduate education and career. Today, when I requested her to understand my crisis, she said she did not trust me and that she believed her father's words.

'I want you to listen to me and understand me. What you saw was real but not the truth. You should hear about me from me. I don't need medicines. It's enough if you understand my agony as my daughter and as a woman,' I said in a trembling voice.

'Mummy, you're talking as if it's a trivial issue. How else would you make me understand your getting caught with your boyfriend in front of daddy and the rest of us? Would you say that he was not your boyfriend but an acquaintance? If he was just an acquaintance, why did he sleep in your bedroom, in your bed like daddy, that too in your lap? Do you realize how we felt, what happened to our reputation and how I would get married? Enough now, didn't the doctor say what happened to you? Take the medicines, get up,' Neha yelled with irritation.

I too yelled out of my fury and grief, 'Then, what about your daddy's girlfriend, your boyfriend, and your younger brother Karthik's girlfriends? What about you? Why is my issue different? I understood you and your daddy. But you have no patience to understand me. Why?'

'How would you and daddy be the same, Mummy? Daddy is a man. You're a woman and a mother, and yet I've to tell you. Do you understand how difficult it is for me? Yes, I know. Daddy really neglected you. But I feel that you shouldn't have done that in retaliation, Mummy.' For some reason, Neha's voice lowered. 'True, even I felt sad when Albert did that. But I did not go with another James to teach him a lesson. Moreover, Mummy, this is not just about relationships. Aren't the heart and love also important?'

Neha was in full flow. I interrupted her, 'Stop, stop. Yes, what you said is correct. It's not just a physical relationship that exists between Madhu and me. Heart and love are important here. Why don't you understand this in my case? Do you apply double moral standards for your Daddy and me just because he's a man? I won't keep quiet if I'm labelled "mad" with these medicines, diagnosed with a disease that I don't have and insulted like this. Go, go away from here.' I snatched the medicines from Neha and threw them out of the window.

The medicines fell right on the face of my husband, Nagesh, who was entering the balcony. That was it – he came into my room like a mad dog, yelling, 'Alivelu'. He caught hold of me, abused me, called me a bitch, and said panting, 'Put the medicines in her mouth. I'll see how she doesn't take the medicines. Alivelu, open her mouth.'

Alivelu swallowed her grief and said, 'Madam, open your mouth to take the medicines.' Nagesh said, 'Would she open her mouth like that?' and forced open my mouth. Neha quickly took two tablets from the strip and put them in my mouth and poured water. My biological son, Karthik, was watching this atrocity through the window. 'Shhh, the nonsense has started again. Won't you let me study at home?'

He shut the window with a bang and left. 'Swallow it,' Nagesh poured some more water into my mouth and made me gulp down the medicines, pushed me onto the bed and left. Neha came to me, saying, 'Mummy,' in a trembling voice, covered me with a blanket and went away. Even in such distress, I noticed that Neha's eyes were wet.

I swallowed tears and humiliation together. When I refused to take the medicines, Nagesh held me by the neck and made me swallow the medicines. The scratches made by his nails on my neck were hurting. I was sprawled on the bed like a strangled pigeon. In that agony, my heart was chanting only one name, Madhu. 'Where are you – you've left me to these cruel people?' I wept quietly. I took out my diary and unconsciously wrote down his name and a few lines...

My eyes are wriggling
like the fish on the banks
drowned in tears
to see you...

How many such songs of separation I wrote! I also wrote about the atrocity I suffered that day. My diary was full of writings after my association with Madhu. I couldn't control my sorrow. I'd slip into a sedated state in half an hour. It would be dawn. I'd wake up drowsily and recollect the dreams of the previous night. Of late, I have been getting repeated dreams, such as my banging on my bedroom doors and running away from home as soon as the doors were open onto the roads and into the forests. Such dreams, like running away from home, started after my marriage with Nagesh.

There was some connection between my dreams and my present condition. Running like that, sometimes I reached Madhu, and sometimes I rushed towards unending green plains and would fall on his lap.

As I lay down reviewing my dreams, Alivelu woke me up. Housework was inevitable. Tea, breakfast and lunch for the three of them…could not breathe till they left. They didn't talk to me. 'Where is this and where is that? Did you pack the lunch box? The shampoo is finished. Did you wipe the dust on the laptop? Did you clean the paint brushes? Why don't you clean the floor properly to remove the colours? Why didn't you talk decently to my friend Ragini the other day? Do you know that she is a great painter and my fan? Isn't it great that she visited the house of a blockhead like you? In any case, how would people like you know about the value of such people? You haven't even completed your postgraduation.' This is how my family members talked to me.

Neha had completed her BTech and was longing to do her MS in a reputed university in America. She was preparing for the GRE. Her father had to spend about ten lakh rupees for that. What did the mother have? Karthik was also treading the same path. Nagesh provided them laptops and mobile phones, and paid their mobile bills and expenses in pubs and clubs. They too knew about their father's waywardness. His relationships with his many girlfriends, my quarrels, my tears, my crossing the threshold several times and then returning, thinking of my small children or parents, and my brother almost beating me up and sending me back…how many times did all these things happen? The same children are saying that they had nothing to do with my suffering and loss, and that I shouldn't have done what I did, carrying on their eyebrows the maturity that they did not have. Do all the children in this world support their fathers because they fulfil their economic needs, irrespective of their rights and wrongs? Was it the inability to protest or was it selfishness? I didn't know.

Neha conceived not once but twice but the fellow she loved and trusted refused to marry her and finally escaped to Dubai with another girl. Wasn't it I who got her abortion done, sheltered her in my bosom and brought her out of depression? I didn't do anything great. It was my responsibility. But today, am I not in the same condition? Where was her compassion for me? Neha did not even have the patience to listen to me about my emotional crisis. Perhaps she was scared of her father not sending her to America if she supported me. Heart-wrenching pain, for some reason. Is it necessary to be worldly wise all the time? Definitely not. But, there it is. This is the reality. Karthik, my son. When I questioned him about the condoms in his pocket, he said that was the fashion of the day. He had relationships with two or three. He rebelled when I slapped him. I made him go for the HIV test, took him to a therapist for counselling. I could see change in him.

How I struggled with these people! As soon as I passed my MA first year, my parents got me married to Nagesh, saying it was a good alliance, he was an upcoming artist and a government employee. I was very fond of Telugu literature.

Although I read Kodavatiganti Kutumbarao, Chalam and Ranganayakamma, I could not escape from slavery. I wanted to write my story some day…

I'd certainly write that! Added to my slavery were Nagesh's bad habits, alcoholism, smoking the hookah and sleeping with other women. It was only if he had all these would he get the inspiration to draw pictures. He frequently brought home some models. He drew them half-naked sometimes and completely naked at other times. If I objected to having the art room at home, he would give me a nasty grin, 'My house, my wish. Either you go away, or else you pose like those women. In any case, you are a mother of two. Where is the sprightliness in you? It's gone.' Wretched fellow! How many times I swept away his brushes, paints, papers and the condoms stinking of his semen, controlling myself from throwing up! Unable to clean up all that, I ran away to my parents but returned, thinking of my children. I repeatedly got the HIV tests done, fearing that I might get AIDS from my husband and that my children might be orphaned.

What was left for me except grief and loneliness? I used to read literature and make serious attempts to write, and would give up abruptly, unable to write. Once Nagesh saw those papers and cackled, saying, 'You are not fit to write.' I felt nauseated. After that, I did not even try to write. I lost interest in life, ended up cooking for him and his guests, watching and standing witness to those people drawing pictures in a spacious, secret art room in a corner of this house and the rubbing of their bodies later.

Sometimes they organized stupid art exhibitions and wet parties for which important people would be invited home. Writers, painters, artists – both men and women – used to come. The wretched ones would drink, have intellectual discussions, throw up in the garden after excessive drinking. They would compare 'this fellow' with world-famous artists, such as Diego Rivera, Renato Guttuso and Hussain Saab, and call him the Andhra Picasso as he fed them and supplied them endless drinks. This fellow would be provoked by such comments, and would drink and dance to the loud music. There are artists who have drawn nudity in all its dignity. But he was not that kind. He drew giving prominence to the male and female private parts. His dark room was full of such pictures. That's why I cleaned his room in a hurry and came out as fast as I could.

That atmosphere was dreadful. In a way, the children were misled by Nagesh's bohemian lifestyle. He was nice to them when he was not drunk. He was concerned about their education and gave them the money that they asked for and bought everything that they wanted. It was Nagesh who encouraged both of them to pursue their studies in America. It was only me who remained dumb. My self-esteem began to crumble in those conditions. Nagesh's constant ridiculing made me angry. For about fifteen days a month, Nagesh would go out of station for camps. I was alone at home – terribly lonely. I longed for companionship. In that loneliness, I tried to spend time in Nagesh's art room. That room would be closed most of the time as the naked pictures might be embarrassing for the visitors. That room would be filled with complete darkness. Slowly, the nudity was revealed. I could not understand what he wanted to say through that nudity. I'd think for long. All the time, he drew pictures of men's and women's genitals and sexual intercourse. Perhaps he wanted to reveal the secrets of creation. Wretched fellow, he didn't know how to make tender love with his wife. It was unbearable for me when the features of the visiting models became clearer in those pictures. Once I came out of that room, there were domestic chores, cooking and children, as usual!

Same loneliness! Was that my life! Did I take birth to play my roles as mother and wife, face abuse and humiliation, fulfil their needs and serve these three throughout my life? 'I'm an artist – an artist. Show me who else is as great an artist as I am in this Andhradesa. Would you compete with me? You hate to cook for me. I was born to draw pictures, and you were born to sweep the garbage around my pictures,' – Nagesh's drunken dialogues. Was that true? Yes, Nagesh was born to draw pictures. Neha and Karthik were born to become engineers. What about me? Was I born to become a slogging mother and wife to make them engineers and artists? Probably yes. Why probably, certainly yes. Hadn't the past twenty-six years pass in this drudgery? Sleep was enveloping me. The poem that I had written longing for Madhu faded out. 'Madam, have you slept?' Alivelu was appointed to guard against my meeting Madhu and prevent Madhu from coming home. Alivelu was paid a salary of four thousand rupees a month and provided food by Nagesh.

'Alivelu, did you ever fall in love?' I slipped into sleep even as I was asking that question of Alivelu.

It was dawn. I cooked with Alivelu's help and sent those three out. I told Alivelu to eat. She said with affection, 'You eat madam; you have to take medicines.' Some movement in my heart! How did it become immoral if Madhu expressed love similar to what Alivelu had for me. I said, 'I am not hungry, Alivelu,' and picked up the diary again. My diary means Madhu's memories. Don't know how he came into my life. With his footprints that crossed skies, oceans, deserts and the entire globe, up to my home and into my heart, as my witness, I didn't know who Madhu was. I didn't know where he came from. I never asked him.

It was one month since I had seen Madhu. Didn't know how and where he was. I tried to recollect his face. Although his form was clear in my imagination, I was not able to recollect his facial features. It is said that if the person you have loved with your heart and soul is distanced, you can really not see his form. His face could not be recollected as clearly as the memories were. It became true in Madhu's case. Sometimes I got angry with Madhu and started to cry. Would he also be crying for me like this? Don't know why, hatred was springing up from my inability to forget him. I wrote like this on my psychological condition:

You made yourself
Audible and visible to me
After ages
When it was not the right time

51

You raised in me
Love for you
Separation that cannot reach you
And tears
Oh moon
I hate you…!

My diary also had a prescription by Dr Ravindra, a famous psychiatrist in the city. He concluded that I had a psychosexual disease called nymphomania and that's why I had a relationship with Madhu, that too, in my middle age (forty-two years), and said that the disease could be cured in one year if I took the four medicines he prescribed. He also blabbered, 'Che, shameless. What is this behaviour at this age, when you have a good husband and grown up children? Behave yourself. Take these medicines, and you will be all right.'

That night I asked Nagesh, 'What disease do I have that I need to take these medicines?'

'You're a sex maniac. These medicines are to cure that disease.' He was curt. That idiot looked at me as if he was looking at a despicable thing, the same way as I make faces when I see him and his used condoms in his dark art room.

'I'm not a sex maniac. I don't want these medicines.' I flung the medicines away. That was it – blows on my back. From then on, he tied up my legs and hands and made me swallow medicines. I searched the dictionary for the meaning of nymphomania. At one place, it said *apsara* (heavenly nymph). I was not an apsara, anyway. When I continued to search, I found that nymphomaniac means a woman who is a sex maniac, a promiscuous woman who has an excessive sexual desire and sleeps with multiple men, a prostitute and a bitch. I had a black-out for a moment. My body trembled with rage and humiliation. That fellow romanced Ragini, Mohini and Kamini in his dark art room at home throughout the day. When they were not there or when they did not come, he fell on me, though I was curling up with hatred, and finished with it, abusing me as frigid. My body did not respond to his touch. In fact, I shuddered as if insects were crawling on my body. Was I ever happy in my twenty-one years of family life with him? I gave birth to children without experiencing any pleasure. In any case, is it necessary to feel pleasure to give birth to children? No, damn it. Am I a nymphomaniac? Nagesh had sexual relations with many. Yet, he was a normal sexual being, not a nymphomaniac. How atrocious! What kind of morality is this? It's only a woman who can be excessively sexual, it seems. What name do they have for men who have an excessive craving for sex? I searched the dictionary. Couldn't find any word. I searched the internet with trembling fingers. No, I couldn't find one. The only words mentioned were hypersexuality and satyriasis. What a respectable name. Who is that fellow who named people like this? My forehead was splitting. Until Nagesh came in the evening, I was striding like a tiger.

That wretched fellow came. Of late, he had been reaching home early, may be due to the Madhu scare. I tore the prescription into pieces, flung them on his face and spat at him. 'You're a gentleman even if you slept with a hundred women, like Ragini and Mohini, at home. Even if I was friends with one – even if I slept with him – did I become a sex maniac for you and that doctor fellow? I don't agree. This diagnosis is wrong. I don't have excessive sexual desires. I don't agree with this doctor and his treatment.' I screamed like mad and held him by his shirt collar.

I pounced on him, beating him and screaming, 'How many men did you see me sleeping with like a sex maniac in these twenty years?' I collapsed and started to knock my legs and hands as if I had hysteria. They hospitalized me. This time, I was diagnosed with hysterical neurosis as well. Two medicines were added. Do I have nymphomania? I felt weak as dead. I couldn't bear this shocking allegation and swallowing the medicines as if to make the allegations true. Did I not say that I would write a story in the future based on this diary? My readers should also believe this story. I don't have sexual desires at all. I never responded to Nagesh's touch. When he forced me, I surrendered my body. After that, he slept satiated and I was left with a headache because of having had to bear that bodyache. But Madhu's memory itself made my heart and body respond. True. One memory – his smile and his fond looks at me, carved lips, sharp nose, brown complexion. Not a toned, muscular body. He looked ordinary, with grey hair here and there and a lean body. He might be above forty years like me. Whatever aspect of him I thought of, my body throbbed. When he touched me, my entire body became a flower of desire and swooned in a violent cyclone. You might think I am shameless. But this is true. The romantic responses my body experienced after the age of forty-two…

A butterfly is
Madly moving about in the room
Yes of course,
The flower of my body on the bed
Is emanating the fragrance of separation!

The first love of my life at the age of forty-two! Didn't know what to do with that joy, fervour, intoxication, craziness every minute… Some throbbing moments when I thought of Madhu but tinged with some fear. I was a married woman with two grown-up children. I should have been guarding my teenage children from falling into the lure of some attraction. Why was I introduced to my first love like this? Was it wrong, immoral? Why? Was it against the scriptures? We should ask a woman biochemical scientist. The hormones of romance in my body responded when I met a man I liked after so many years. Did they make a mistake? Or was something wrong with me? But, my mind did not agree with this. It was accepting the reality and experiencing it. Did my heart and body ever respond to many men, like the doctor and Nagesh said? Wasn't it only to my dearest Madhu that I responded? You tell me.

'Madam, you have to take medicines. Have breakfast,' Alivelu alerted me. Alivelu never insulted me. As if she had understood me, she explained, 'Why these unnecessary quarrels with the master, madam? These men fellows can do anything and get away. But if we women even smile sometimes, we become bitches. Take care of your health and children.' The same old moral principle preached in this world for ages was once again being explained in detail.

I couldn't escape from Alivelu's warnings. I had breakfast. I pretended to have taken the medicines, went into the toilet and spat them out, like I always do. Why should I take those medicines? Who should be taking the medicines, Nagesh or me?

I went out and sat in the balcony. Wasn't this the balcony that had brought the doom on me and introduced me to Madhu? I couldn't bear the memories of Madhu that surrounded me and my overflowing tears. I had to take sedatives to bear that intense pain. Added to that, the doctor called me a nymphomaniac and made me a prostitute. Sex workers also have a morality, a social perspective and a heart. That word was turned into an abuse and attributed to the excessive working of the hormones in a woman's body. Wasn't it criminal to do that? My condition was not even that. Comparing my proximity with Madhu to promiscuity and saying that I had excessive sexual desires – was unbearable for me.

I opened a magazine to divert my attention. An article in that magazine appealed to me. A marital therapist, Dr Manoja, argued that women's psychological and sexual problems are not personal, but that their roots are to be found in the social and political institutions around us and that we should search for solutions in the same. She had been researching women's sexual problems for the past few years and writing articles in journals. Many a time, after reading her article in the past, I had thought of going to her to discuss Nagesh's obsession with women and his sexual perversion and also, get him counselled by her. But now that I am said to have that wretched disease, I want to know all about it. I believed Dr Manoja would counsel Nagesh along with me. Of course, Nagesh would be more than happy to send me for counselling. Wasn't it usual for men to ascribe all kinds of physical and psychological ailments to women and degrade them? I might have to stay with the doctor for a week, and I was ready to do that.

'You HAVE TO LISTEN to my entire story. I came to you for clarity on one issue. AM I A NYMPHOMANIAC? Am I a woman with excessive sexual desires? Am I a bitch? On what basis did that psychiatrist decide on my condition, believing my husband's version? My husband has never paid that kind of fees to anyone. Do you know how much he paid? He gave a cheque for fifty thousand rupees. Why did he give so much money? Tell me. Am I a nymphomaniac? I am not, am I?

'You read my diary the whole of yesterday. Tell me. Didn't your questionnaire reveal that my psychological condition is balanced and has not lost stability? Tell me,' my voice was trembling. My lips were parched and my body was sweating. I was like someone who had resolved to achieve success, whether it was by dying in war or killing the enemy. I was enraged, like a rough sea, like a valiant soldier, tortured by the enemy who had left her thinking that she was dead, coming back to consciousness, gathering the last drop of blood and getting ready to jump into the battle, as if believing that somehow the night of the cyclone had to be spent and pacified.

'No, I am not a nymphomaniac. Doctor, at least you tell me. How dare that doctor fellow say that? That fellow…' I clenched my teeth and fists in anger. Don't know what would have happened if those two fellows were in front of me!

My sorrow, the sounds of my grief were like the struggle of a scapegoat who had justice on her side but had to succumb to the conspiracy of the enemy. The doctor couldn't control her tears when the helpless screams of grief emanated from my voice and when I crumbled lamenting. But the counsellor had to keep calm. I kept crying, openly, so intensely as if the heart would jump out and I would not get the opportunity to weep again. My wailing started all of a sudden, and it stopped equally abruptly. My face became calm like an angry ocean, which roared in a commotion, ran forward in dreadful waves and later fell, withdrew backwards, subsided and quietened down.

The doctor was quiet for a while. Then she cajoled me, 'Would you tell me about Madhu?' I said, 'Yes, I didn't tell you everything about Madhu, did I? I'll tell you again from the beginning. I'll tell you about what I did not write in my diary,' my face changed. My swollen face reddened further. My lips opened and there was a glow of immense joy on my face. My eyes were shining like leaves in the sunlight. Did even the memory of a person one loved fill one's face with such beauty? I was reminded of Ghalib's verse which said that one can escape from any guilt without being detected, but one can't escape being discovered when in love.

For some reason, the doctor was observing me intently. She probably thought I was good-looking, of a desirable height and weight, and with a dusky complexion and shining eyes. Not great beauty, but amusing beauty.

'I'm at home throughout the day after Nagesh and the children leave. Nagesh started keeping a distance after my attachment to him waned. Rarely had sex. Once in two months. Didn't I tell you that he remembered me when his friends didn't turn up? I endured that ten-minute hell either by closing my eyes or by refusing it. I lost interest in continuing my postgraduate studies. Reading stories, watching TV, eating, making tea for myself after the afternoon siesta and sitting in the balcony and sipping it, watching the passers-by, listening to my favourite ghazals by Rafi, Mukesh, Jagjit Singh and Ghulam Ali – these became my addictions.

'The children came home between seven and eight in the evening, after their tuition. The flowering plants in my garden, songs, evenings, my tea, the strangers I saw during evening walks were my friends. Madhu was one such stranger. He used to pass by my house during his evening walk every day, in white pyjamas and with neatly combed hair. I did not bother about him much in the beginning. But I felt as if he looked at me with great interest when he walked in front of my house. That generated interest in me. Seeing him every day and watching him staring at me became a habit for me. Again in half an hour, he would return, looking at me. Soon, Madhu became an obsession for me, like Rafi's songs. If he did not come on a certain day, I waited for him in anticipation. I'd spend sleepless nights sitting on the balcony, staring at the road that carried his footsteps. The following day when he came, the streams of blood would surge up from my heart and flow through my body, submerging me and leaving me astonished. Perhaps he noticed the joy on my face – he smiled. I felt humiliated caught like that.

'Sometimes I hid behind the curtain in the living room. His eyes followed our windows as he walked in front of our house and then briskly walked away. On his return, I would be sitting on the balcony like a queen on top of the world! He went away complaining with his eyes that I was not there before. Once, I had to take Neha to Bhopal for some entrance test. I felt sad about not seeing him for four days. But that was a journey I couldn't escape from. I went, but my heart was full of Madhu. By five in the evening, I would think of him searching for me and agonizing over his not being able to see me.

'On the fourth day when I returned, I saw him with an unshaven face, depressed. I felt sad. I knew that our hide and seek game had reached the point where we would not be able to exist without seeing each other and that we were in love. I could clearly understand. Blaming myself for my craziness, I would remain indoors to control myself. Then I would understand how both of us went through hell when we could not see each other, and the balcony phase would begin again. I could feel the enthusiasm, happiness and interest that I had never felt before. Is there such greatness in love? Is love that great? Would love crop up after forty years of age? Which psychiatrist should I ask about the truth? There was a metamorphosis in me. From a caterpillar, I became a butterfly. People and life became beautiful. I would be smiling to myself, thinking of Madhu, and be caught by people at home. An awareness of beauty, which I had never had, started to grow in me. I chose the colours I wore so that they would suit me. Light colours suited my dusky complexion. I had a good stature and the right weight. I looked fit, though I was in my forties. I bought creams to make my face look better. Like never before in my life, I went to the beauty parlour for facials and became someone even I could not recognize. Nagesh and the children noticed the change in me, but did not bother much. I saw the glow in Madhu's eyes when I looked beautiful and felt ecstatic. I never felt that ecstasy when Nagesh would touch me; he would completely envelop me in lust. Think what you will, Nagesh's behaviour was not that painful any longer. I had found a treasure trove that was Madhu!

'That day was a turning point in my life. As usual, the children and Nagesh went away at nine-thirty in the morning. I was cleaning the house. The main door was open. A knock on the door. I went to see who it was. Madhu! He came in and bolted the door. I was awestruck. He came close to me, showered my face and neck with kisses and took me towards the bedroom. I remained stunned. He enveloped me.

61

'Slowly, he placed my night dress on me. I recovered and wore the night dress. He took my palm into his hands and kissed it. He hugged me to his heart, kissed me on my forehead, and asked, looking deep into my eyes, "My name is Madhu. What is your name?"

'I said, "Rudra". He said, "Nice name," and left.

'That's how our relationship started. How sensitive and loving his touch was to my body! I can't agree that he felt only lust. He felt ecstatic touching my ears with his lips and whispering, "Rudra, my love." He asked, "Rudra my life, have you come after so long?"

'How lovingly he touched every inch of my body! Sometimes he talked and touched me like a mother whose love for her child was overflowing. I used to touch Neha and Karthik when they were children with such affection and hug them to my heart. Madhu kissed my feet with his lips and pressed them to his eyes. The way he put his face to my feet was like saluting a goddess and he whispered, "My dear, my dear." In fact, he made love less and did such things more. I too was in a similar condition. I felt as if my life was blessed by his touch. I melted into tears in his love. I couldn't expect any love from Nagesh even in my dreams. Nagesh never touched me with such love. He pounced on me and squeezed my body. I surrendered to Madhu's tender love.

'Who gave me so much love? My husband did not. If I went to my parents and brothers, since my husband was going around with other women and beating me like a beast, they almost beat me and drove me away. My grown-up children never treated me with such love. They were immersed in their careers.

'We rarely made love. He slept with his head in my lap or he made me sleep with my head in his lap. How lovingly he stroked my head! Nagesh never did that. I felt like crying when he left. He said, "Crazy thing, won't I come back?"

'Until I saw him the following day, I would go crazy with loneliness. Waves of excitement rose in me when he came. My body and mind had never experienced such happiness. I did not know how to thank Madhu for familiarizing me with it. The love-making between us was also great. For the first time, I came to understand how happiness becomes a surging wave that reaches the body and mind to the shore and how great it is when two bodies meet in great attraction, in longing and burning desire. Love-making came on its own along with the attraction and love I felt for Madhu. Love-making did not unite me with Madhu, but attraction and love did. I did not regret anything or feel scared or guilty. I felt it was the right relationship and that the relationship between Nagesh and me was illicit and immoral. I felt as if all other relationships in this world were unreal, except our love. I never asked him about his name, where he came from, his house and family. Somehow, I felt these are things that everyone in this world has. He too did not ask me any questions. It pricked me when I thought that he was cheating on his wife, if he had one, like Nagesh cheated on me. Sometimes I wondered if this was my answer to Nagesh's dark art room affairs. Once I tried to ask him, but he said, "Please, don't ask me about that. You, me, love and these moments are the only reality."

'That was the most unfortunate day in my life. Nagesh, Neha and Karthik all came home unexpectedly at the same time. He had his head in my lap. We were enjoying Rafi's excellent song, "*Baharon phool barsao, mera mehboob aayaa hai* (Seasons, shower the flowers, my lady love has arrived)."

'Suddenly the air froze. All three of them were staring like mad. Madhu quickly got up, quietly pressed my hand and left. You know the story after that, don't you doctor? Nagesh's ego was severely hurt. His boorish behaviour worsened.

'"What did you see in that fellow?" he asked me again and again. I said, "Love." He bashed me up, saying, "Don't I have it, you woman! Isn't this house and all these cars for you?"

'He got drunk and yelled madly, "Did you have sex? How many times? You bitch, tell me." I said yes. He got worse and kicked my ribs and banged my head against the wall till it bled. Even then, I thought of Madhu. Once Nagesh was drunk and ran after me to cut my hair. Somehow I escaped.'

'Tell me, doctor, am I a nymphomaniac?' I asked. There was a strange glow on my face. The grief and pain of the past were no longer there.

'No Rudra, you are not a nymphomaniac. That was a wrong diagnosis,' said the doctor.

I smiled like a child and said, 'I know, I know that I'm not a nymphomaniac.' My face fell and my head drooped to one side. I looked expectantly into the doctor's eyes. 'Then, was my relationship with Madhu wrong? I know that it was not wrong, but if you also say the same…' The doctor said, 'What happened to you was not wrong. The conditions that pushed you into that situation were wrong.'

My face bloomed. 'Doctor, I like and love Madhu very much.'

The doctor's eyes became wet and she kept looking at me with a smile, 'What's wrong with loving and experiencing that love?'

I smiled again and said, 'They forcibly give me these medicines every morning. I'm throwing them away,' I said, showing her the bunch of tablet strips in my purse.

She told me to throw them into the dustbin. I got up, saying, 'If we have to, shouldn't we give them to Nagesh? A diagnosis and medicines worth fifty thousand rupees.' I guffawed, threw the tablets into the dustbin.

The doctor asked me, 'What happened to Madhu? Where is he?'

'I don't know. I don't know who he was, where he came from and where he went. A love affair with an unknown person seems strange, but it was true. Once I pleaded with Alivelu, went out and anxiously searched the lanes and parks. I could not see Madhu. I don't miss Madhu so much now. I'm surprised. But I'm really thankful to him for what he gave me. If ever I run into him on the road or in the park, I won't abuse him but will only thank him. He himself did not know the value of what he gifted me.' My voice choked. The doctor seemed surprised at my confidence. I stayed with the doctor for two days.

My husband and children arrived.

Nagesh asked, 'Will my wife be cured of the disease, doctor?'

The doctor said, 'Your wife does not have any disease. You do.'

With a mix of surprise and anger, he said, 'Doctor, your diagnosis is wrong.'

'No, you have nymphomania.' The doctor explained how he was a nymphomaniac.

He kept listening to her. Didn't he know? The children and Nagesh spent three days in the counselling centre. As we were leaving, Neha said with tears in her eyes, 'Sorry doctor, I should have become her mother and consoled her. I behaved worse than an enemy.' That was enough for me. Nagesh was a nymphomaniac. It would take some time for him to change.

I returned home. Now, I had my balcony, my garden and Rafi's song with me as usual and also a few things that had joined this list – new literature, white paper and a pen to write down my feelings as and when I wished to. To write my story too. Alivelu was not beside me. Madhu would always stay with me. The touch of Madhu's final handshake had not left me yet!

§

five

Stone

'No, I won't go.' Seventeen-year-old Asra insisted, shaking her head in refusal. Her face bore fear and contempt for the man who came for her.

'Come on, it's your father. You always go, don't you? What happened to you today? Your mother is unwell, it seems. Go for two days – then come back,' warden Rukhiya Begum scolded her. Abbajan Khadri, fifty years old, looked daggers at his daughter and growled at her, 'Let's go.' Asra walked behind her Abba, tears welling up in her eyes, a small bag of clothes in her hand; like a lamb behind the slaughterer.

Khadri got her into an autorickshaw. The auto rushed forward. Asra started crying, 'I won't go there. I'll go to Ammi.'

'Don't cry. Am I a stranger? Keep quiet.' Khadri tried to hush the sobbing girl. Fearing that the auto fellow might suspect something, he pinched Asra's thigh hard. Asra was about to scream but contained that shriek, as well as her grief, within herself. The auto weaved its way through several lanes and, after one hour, halted in front of a door in a basti, a slum-like neighbourhood.

Khadri opened the lock and chided Asra to go in. She quietly entered the small room. There was no furniture, except a mat. Khadri closed the door and pushed Asra, who was pleading, 'No, Abba, no!' He threw her onto the mat and slapped her hard. 'It has been going on for the past ten years. Why do you act as if it's new for you every time? You have become my beevi (wife). You're my wife.' He occupied Asra with a crooked laugh.

After an hour, smoking a beedi, he asked Asra, 'Are you hungry?' Asra shook her head to say no. She sat curled up like a wounded pigeon, leaning against the door. 'Wait, I'll get something to eat. Don't think of running away. I've a fellow on guard outside.' Crushing the beedi under his chappals, he walked out.

Asra bolted the door, went into the bathroom and wept. She sat down under the tap to wash away the filth that her father had rubbed on her. When would she escape from this cruel, mean thing that her Abba, her biological father, was doing to her? Who would save her from this haivan abba (devilish father)? What if she died, or told Sameena madam? She should tell Sameena madam. That madam was really good. She would save her. She had asked her several times, 'What happened Asra? Why are you looking so dull? What happened, child, won't you tell me?' But Asra was too scared to tell her anything. She felt deeply ashamed and insulted. Everyone asked, 'Why are you scared? You are only going to your Ammi with your Abba.' But little did they know about what Abba did to her. He would take her to some unknown place after telling the warden that Ammi was not well. He would keep Asra there for a week and have sex with her.

Why was this happening only to her? Did any other biological father do such a thing with his own children? Did the abbas of her friends Raziya, Khaisar, Fathima, Rani and Mary do such things with their children? They didn't. She knew it was a sin. Nowhere in this world would it be like this. The haivan abba who could say 'you are my beevi' to his daughter did not exist. God wouldn't forgive him. He wouldn't forgive her either, who was enduring the relationship with her own father. She was a sinner. Asra wept for a long time, banging her head against the wall while taking a bath and repeating, 'God, don't forgive me, punish me.' Despite the long bath, the dreadful, sinful sticky feeling between her legs wouldn't go. She asked god to take her life.

ASRA'S VOICE WAS SHAKING. She asked slowly but clearly, 'Madam, will god forgive someone who has a relationship with one's biological father?' Sameena teacher, who was correcting students' notebooks, felt a chill run down her spine. She collected herself to ask, 'Asra, do you understand the meaning of what you said? Are you at all in your senses? No god will ever accept such a relationship. It's a wrong relationship.'

'No madam, I'm fully conscious of what I am asking you. One of my friends is facing this problem. She lives in our lane. She asked me when I went home last time. I told her I'll check with my teacher.' Asra faltered, and tears flowed down her cheeks. There was something – the girl was hiding something. Sameena looked intently at Asra's face. There were dark circles under Asra's eyes, like black rain clouds, with the eyelids shut, as if she was bearing some secret grief.

Those tender lips were trembling. Asra bent her head low, laden with grief for committing a blunder. Sameena teacher wondered if her father was doing something to her and she was shaken at the thought.

'Asra, will you come to my house today? I've to talk to you.' Asra nodded her head in agreement.

AFTER DINNER THAT NIGHT, Sameena sat down with Asra and asked calmly, 'Tell me Asra, who is that friend? Is that you? Tell me, I can understand. Tell me the truth.' She gently stroked Asra's shoulder. Like a melting cloud, Asra collapsed on Sameena teacher, crying. Sameena did not utter a word, and let her cry. Asra recovered and said, 'Yes madam, I'm that unfortunate, mean sinner.' Sameena was quiet; her doubt was confirmed. She couldn't hold back her tears. Sameena was speechless. She, who had seen life closely, didn't know what to say. Her heart froze.

Asra started to narrate her story and Sameena listened to her with bated breath. Asra spoke in a low voice, 'I had two abortions. Abba gave me some tablets. Once when the abortion did not happen even ten days after taking the tablets, he took me to the room and forcibly had sex with me five or six times through the night. He squeezed below the lower abdomen. Finally, he called a midwife who put a wood-like piece inside; it expanded inside, and I wept through the night with pain. I fell at his feet begging him to remove it. He beat me up severely. After a long spell of pain, the foetus fell by the next morning.' On her face could be seen the detachment of a person who had died bearing pain and suffering. Was Asra speaking after death? Had she become a corpse unable to die, shuttling between life and death? Sameena's heart fluttered with fear. She closed her ears with shame, not to hear about the horrid incidents. She hugged Asra to her bosom and wept.

SAMEENA TEACHER'S ELDER daughter, seventeen-year-old Zakhia, was throwing a tantrum, refusing to eat. Her abba was feeding her, 'Just a little, it's over; please eat, my dear.' Zakhiya was writing her annual examinations. She was studying Intermediate at a local college. Asra was staring at Zakhiya's father. So much love on his face!

Asra was reminded of her Abba, Khadri. Suddenly, fear crawled down her spine like a centipede. Did her abba ever look at her like that, with such love in his eyes? His looks would fondle her whole body, with desire and lust in his red eyes. She would curl up, cover her body with her chunni and try to escape from his looks, slip into some room, the kitchen, or loiter here and there. He would come to her on some pretext and secretly touch her breasts. He would order her to press his legs, and as she was doing that, he would put his legs on her lower abdomen. Asra became bitter once again.

Mazhar Ali noticed Asra watching them and said, 'Come beti, you also eat.' The hidden grief surged up in Asra when he addressed her as beti (daughter). She said, 'No, sir,' and ran into another room. Pain enveloped Mazhar's heart. He wanted to bring her close to him endearingly. But he was scared to even look at the wounded Asra.

Sameena cleaned up the kitchen and went into Zakhiya's room. Zakhiya was tense about her studies and exams. Zakhiya was Sameena's future dream. She wanted to become a doctor. She studied day and night and was confident that she would get a seat in a medical college. Sameena had studied in a madarsa. She had studied, but not the way she would have liked. Her father had brought her up under strict regulations. He had not sent her to school despite her desire to do so. Her education had ended in a madarsa and she had a command over Arabic and Persian. She wanted her daughter not to become like her.

Sameena peeped into Asra's room. She was absorbed in writing something in a book. She closed the book and smiled feebly when she saw Sameena. Sameena went up to her and asked, 'What are you writing, Asra?' Asra put the book in Sameena's hand. Written all over the book, a million times, was 'God forgive me.' Sameena's eyes became wet. It seemed Asra had been writing like that since her childhood, from the time she realized what her Abba was doing to her and from the time she understood that it was sinful.

'Asra, you have not committed any sin. Your Abba has. God will definitely punish him and send him to hell. Your Abba is in jail; he will be given a big punishment. Don't weep. It's already late into the night. Sleep now.' Sameena covered her with a blanket and left the room.

SAMEENA WENT INTO her room and lay down, but could not sleep. Asra's words rang in her ears, 'Yes madam, I am that mean person, the one who has an illicit relationship with my biological father. God won't forgive me. He will certainly send me to hell. I want to die, madam.' Sameena's blood boiled but she didn't know what to do. When she had spoken to Asra about going to the police, Asra was frightened. 'No, no, he will kill my mother and me. He bashed Ammi several times so hard that she could have died.' She showed a burn scar on her thigh and said, 'He is a haivan, not a human. Don't report to the police, madam.'

Sameena asked with anger and pain, 'Tell me, will you bear this throughout your life? He will do this as long as he is alive. You've been bearing it for ten years now. How long can this go on?'

'I'll pray to god. He will take care of everything,' said Asra with a broken heart.

'Think sensibly.' Sameena cajoled her, 'God will take care of everything. But we should also do something, shouldn't we? Does god tell us to bear injustice? How unjust is it on your part to bear such injustice? You are unjust to yourself as well as to the society around you. If you continue to bear it and put the responsibility on god, it will increase your Abba's strength. He won't leave you until he is dead.' Sameena spoke for a long time and finally convinced Asra to think practically. Asra agreed to lodge a complaint in the police station against her Abba. Sameena asked another teacher, Parveen, to go with them to the police station. Parveen listened to Asra's entire story. She said, 'Poor thing. God will never forgive your abba. I pray to god on your behalf that your abba should be punished.' But when it came to going to the police station, Parveen stuttered, 'No, we've a meeting at home today. I've invited friends for dinner. I'm going to speak about humanity in religion. I have to prepare for that.'

Sameena was angry, 'God also said don't tolerate inhumanity and devilish behaviour, didn't you know? We can take our relatives and friends, and all of us women could stage a dharna in front of the police station.'

Parveen mumbled, 'No, no. I won't come, forgive me.'

Sameena was furious.

'Let's go; we don't want anyone to go with us. You and I are enough.' Sameena held Asra's hand and hurried out of the madarsa.

'In any case, this girl silently waited for ten years and tolerated it. How did she suddenly become conscious now? This one also doesn't have sense ...' Parveen was telling someone.

THE POLICE SEARCHED FOR Khadri and caught him. Sameena

looked at Khadri. He looked normal – poor, lean and pathetic. Like her neighbours, he was very plain, but there was haivaniyat (devilish streak) in his eyes. He fumed at Asra. He held the prison bars and screamed, 'I'm innocent. I'm her father. How can I do that? She is lying.'

WOMEN'S ORGANIZATIONS RUSHED IN. Lawyers, psychiatrists and social workers put questions to Asra. She panicked, unable to answer their questions, and wept. She felt demoralized and scared. Everything was published in the newspapers, including photos of Khadri and Asra. The court handed the responsibility of Asra's protection to Sameena for some time. Sameena also participated in dharnas along with the women's organizations. She took her daughter, Zakhiya, and Asra along with her. Asra's Ammi – Khurshid Begum – and Asra's younger sister also participated in dharnas.

AFTER KHADRI HAD BEEN PUT behind bars, Sameena took Asra to her Ammi.

Asra stood outside the house, scared. Sameena took her inside, holding her by the hand. A sixteen-year-old boy rushed in, pulled Asra by the hair and battered her back, shouting, 'You bitch, you sent Abba to jail. I'll kill you.' Asra's Ammi released her from Ameed. Asra collapsed, weeping. Ameed was Asra's younger brother, just two years younger. Ameed went in, looking sharply at Asra and Sameena. People in the locality, particularly his friends, laughed at the family. That was humiliating for Ameed. He was furious that Asra had made a domestic issue public instead of keeping it a secret.

Asra stopped crying, went up to her Ammi, put her hand on her Ammi's shoulder and said, 'Ammi, forgive me. You run away from here, else Abba will kill you.'

Khurshid Begum hugged her daughter and said, 'You have to forgive me, my child.' Tears welled up in Sameena's eyes seeing the mother and the daughter. She did not have the heart to console them, and let them weep. She looked around the house – in three small rooms eight children had to live. They were all looking at her, scared. They did not understand anything. They heard from people in the locality that Abba was in jail and Asra Apa (elder sister) was responsible for that. They didn't know why. Fifteen-year-old Ruksana knew about it. Ruksana was feeding roti to her six-year-old sister and her thoughts lingered on the times she had seen him putting his hands inside the panties of her six-year-old sister, Tayyaba. She could understand how much torture that fellow would have subjected Asra to. Ammi also knew. Ruksana gave the plate to Tayyaba and hugged Asra, anguished.

A woman rushed in from the next room like a cyclone and almost pounced on Asra, as if to beat her, 'You've ruined the family honour. You sent him to jail. Would you look after my children?'

Khurshid Begum got up and pushed her away. 'I'll kill you if you touch my daughter.' That woman fell on the floor. Her children surrounded her. Beating her chest, she wailed, 'O god, how does one live with these children? Ammi–beti have sent behind bars the man who feeds us.' Sameena could understand that she was Khadri's second wife, Hafeeza. She too had five children. The eldest, fourteen-year-old daughter, Shabana, was looking at her mother with teary eyes and was consoling her younger brothers and sisters.

Sameena looked at Asra, 'Shall we go?' Khurshid Begum intervened, 'I'll send her after two days. Nothing will happen. That haivan is in jail, isn't it! I'll guard her against my son, Ameed.' Sameena hesitated, but Asra said, 'I'll stay with Ammi for two days, madam, please.'

Sameena briefed her on being cautious. She gave her mobile phone to Asra and told her to call twice a day. Those two days, people in the locality invaded Asra's house to 'see' her. Khurshid Begum did not open the door. One night, stones were pelted on their house. Asra's family spent that night in fear. One stone fell on Ameed, who was returning home, and injured him. The fellow yelled at his mother, 'First kick this woman out and send her to that Sameena teacher. The court has handed over Asra to her, hasn't it? This woman should not be here, send her away.' Khurshid Begum too shouted back, saying, 'You fellow, she's your sister, not your enemy.' Ameed growled, 'Both of you go to the streets and do dharnas. You too went there, didn't you? All the women in the house can also go along with you.'

THE THIRD DAY, Khurshid Begum went out to drop Asra at Sameena's place. Asra started off with her Ammi, after telling her younger brother and younger sister, 'I'm going. Take care of Ammi,' and wailing uncontrollably. People in the locality gave them strange looks. 'Look, how both Ammi and beti are wandering around without shame!'

'How did she bear all these years?'

'If he was doing it for the past seven years, why reveal it when she is seventeen? It seems mother and daughter were living like rival wives for that Khadri fellow. How shameless that mother must be…how could she keep quiet?' People made comments as Asra and her mother were walking on the road. One man said, 'Shameless women, how could you bring into the streets things meant to be hidden in the house?' and threw a stone. It hit Asra's forehead. Asra collapsed, calling out to her mother. Khurshid Begum cried, 'Please don't throw stones at us, sirs. It's not our fault.We're innocent.' As Khurshid pulled up Asra, another stone fell on her. People pelted stones at them. Khurshid Begum shielded her daughter and ran on the road. Asra's heart blazed with rage against her Abba. His hands and legs should be tied and he should be beaten with those stones until he was dead. She asked Khurshid Begum to stop. Ammi warned, 'We'll die. Run.' Asra picked up the stones pelted on them and started throwing them in all directions, as if in a frenzy. Khurshid Begum, initially stunned, picked up the stones too.

SAMEENA WAS SADDENED to see Asra and Khurshid Begum reach her home wounded. She took them to the doctor. After he took care of their wounds, she asked her husband, Mazhar, to escort Khurshid Begum home safely.

Asra went into a depression. The wounds caused by the stones still ached. Why did people beat them up with stones? Wasn't it Abba who violated his biological daughter? Why did they try to punish her and her mother, instead of Abba? They described Khurshid and Asra as rival wives of Khadri. What if she died, cut her blood vessels with a blade? Asra wept often. She prayed to god all the time to save her from this sin. She couldn't eat well. Asra was already lean and starved, and now she looked like a corpse.

She sat near the window and looked at the sky. Why did this happen to her? Did she make a mistake by tolerating it all those days? Ammi had told her to tell the media persons when they had come to their house when she was thirteen. Ammi had explained to her how to tell the media persons. But she didn't tell them. Abba had threatened her that he would kill Ammi if she opened her mouth. One night Abba was dragging her into the kitchen when Ammi fell on his feet, 'No, leave her, for the fear of god.' Abba bashed her without mercy, tied the sari around her neck and was about to hang her from the ceiling when Asra begged of him, 'No, Abba, I'll do whatever you want me to. Don't kill Ammi.' Only then that haivan abba let Ammi go. He pushed her into the kitchen, without even looking at Ammi, who had fainted by then.

How did Abba start this sinful thing? When Ammi was pregnant with Bashir, he sent Ammi to the hospital frequently for check-ups. Asra was seven years old then. She didn't know anything. Abba would catch hold of her, make her sit in his lap and put his hands in her panties. He wouldn't let her go even though she tried to push him away and struggled to free herself. She stopped going near Abba. When he put his hands in her panties, she felt a burning sensation. Afterwards when she peed, she screamed, 'Ammi, it burns.' Ammi gave her some sugar water. She ran out when Abba came home and went to her Khalajan (aunt). He went there too searching for her. When she continued to weep because of the burning, her Ammi suspected something and took off her panties. She saw a wound and thought it was probably an insect bite and took her to the doctor. The doctor said, 'Khurshid Begum, someone is misbehaving with the child. Find out if any bad boys from your neighbourhood are doing dirty things with her. Be with the child all the time. Don't leave her. Protect her.'

Ammi was heartbroken. She asked Asra and gave her chocolates, but Asra didn't tell her anything. Abba had threatened her that he would kill Ammi and her younger sisters if she told her anything about it. After much persuasion, Asra finally told her that it was Abba. Ammi froze in horror. After that, whenever Abba approached her, Ammi would take her away from there. He understood that Ammi knew about it, and started to bash her more. He threatened to kill her if she prevented him.

Ammi had completed nine months of pregnancy. She refused to go to the hospital and insisted on delivering at home. Ammi had her own fears. Abba did not listen to her. He forcibly sent her to the hospital. That night, Abba did many things with Asra. She writhed, 'Leave me Abba, leave me, I fall at your feet.' He did not listen. He continued, 'No daughter, this is my love.'

Was a father's love like that? Did the father of her neighbourhood friend, Saira, also love her like that? Did love mean squeezing the body like that, biting one's lips and stabbing one between the legs? He threatened her, 'Don't tell Ammi. I'll kill you. I will cut you and your Ammi into pieces.'

He brought some ointment and asked her to apply it when she bled the first time. He gave her some tablets to reduce the pain. Ammi returned from the hospital and noticed that Asra was walking with legs widened. She understood that the atrocity she had been guarding against had taken place. She madly beat her chest, 'Don't go to Abba. Why didn't you run away to Khala's house?'

Asra also wept, 'He threatened to kill you Ammi, that's why I didn't tell you.' Abba came drunk and bashed her up and her Ammi and went to Hafeeza Ammi. Hafeeza Ammi was in the adjacent room. This secret remained between her, Ammi and Abba for a long time. Abba bashed up Ammi like an animal and said, 'Asra is my seed, I have the authority over her. I won't hand her over to some fellow.' Asra turned thirteen and her periods started.

One day, Abba brought jasmine flowers and in Ammi's presence asked Asra to wear them in her hair. She refused; he beat her up. Ammi tried to prevent him; he beat up Ammi too. She quietly wore the flowers in her hair. He laughed, telling Ammi, 'This is my wife.' He pulled her into the kitchen, telling Ammi, 'You are jealous.' He insisted that Asra should serve him food, rub his back when he bathed and be ready in the kitchen as soon as he reached home. Or else he belted her and Ammi.

After he left her at night, Asra came out of the kitchen and slept next to Ruksana. Mother sat like a statue throughout the night. She couldn't bear it any longer and lodged a complaint with the police. The police, media persons and women's organizations came. But Asra told them that Ammi was lying as Abba had married again and that Abba was a good man. They all left, abusing Ammi.

The police warned Ammi not to do such things and went away. That day, Abba broke the bones in Ammi's hands. Ammi ran out of the house with broken hands and fainted. Abba disappeared. Ammi had to stay in Osmania Hospital for a month. Rods were fixed in Ammi's hands. He threatened to mix poison in Ammi's food if Asra informed the police or the media persons. Asra showed that bottle of poison to her Ammi.

Ammi thought through that month and admitted her in a madarsa. Adjacent to the madarsa was a hostel. But Abba returned. He made enquiries and found out where she was. He took her out every now and then. He even insisted, 'You are my wife.' Asra did not tell her Ammi. Ammi might quarrel with him again. She wondered if this time he would break her legs or kill her – he was not scared of anything. Ammi was happy in the false belief that Asra was safe and away from this haivan.

Their house was very small. Moreover, they had to give a room to Hafeeza Ammi and her daughters. The children watched what Abba did with Ammi through the doors, with her and with Hafeeza Ammi taking off his clothes. One night, her brother, Ameed, two years younger than her, tried to do what Abba did with her and she screamed. Ammi woke up and bashed him up. The fellow asked her, 'Isn't it wrong if Abba does it?' Ammi collapsed with shame and grief. He went away, saying that he wouldn't contribute a single rupee to the home. After that, he stayed outside with friends. During the day, he worked in a footwear shop and earned fifteen hundred rupees per month.

Abba was sleeping, drunk. He would probably feel happy that his son had also become a man, like him, if he learnt about it. Asra was reminded of all this. Although she came out of that hell-like house to the hostel, she could not escape from the venomous bites of her Abba. She wailed with deep grief.

Sameena held Asra's hands and asked, 'What happened Asra? Tell me.' Asra struggled to say something but couldn't because of shame and pain. When Sameena forced her, Asra said, 'Pain in the stomach and back, white discharge, some burning blisters between the legs.' Sameena felt a stabbing pain in her heart. She didn't know what diseases that haivan abba had passed on to her.

THE GYNAECOLOGIST, Dr Kaneez Begum, recognized Asra and Sameena. She had read about them in the newspapers.

The court had also sent Asra to her for a gynaecological examination to find out about her Abba's haivaniyat. Apart from her, senior gynaecologists also examined her. It was found that Asra was subjected to sexual atrocities. They wrote this in the reports.

As she was examining the young girl, who was like a fragrant flower dying with humiliation, cajoling her and making her lie down on the table, tears welled up in the doctor's eyes. Asra froze with fear, calling out 'O god' as the speculum was inserted between her legs. Men go around as they wish and pass on their dreadful venereal diseases to innocent wives. The gynaecologist had examined women who tolerated such husbands and came to her weeping, and had prescribed medicines to them for their husbands' stinking venereal diseases. She drew out their blood for examination. Husbands didn't come and didn't get the tests done. They said they had no problem. Her medicines might cure the wives' diseases. But their husbands continued to have untreated diseases. So the wives contracted the diseases again and came again to the gynaecologist. Criminal cases should be filed against men who spread terrible venereal diseases to their wives, and who escape from treatment and push their wives towards an untimely death, and against men who hide their diseases and get married.

She advised the wives, 'Why do you put up with such husbands? Threaten them, leave them, lodge a complaint with the police as well as the women's organizations.' But that day she couldn't bear to look at the venereal diseases that a father had spread to his daughter, as her tears were blocking her vision. She examined Asra, prescribed medicines and said, 'There is a high level of infection. Let her get the tests done. Meanwhile, use these tablets and ointments.' She told Sameena, 'Take Asra to a psychologist; she is in a deep depression.' Sameena agreed. She had also been thinking of taking Asra to a psychologist after noticing her weep every now and then.

THIS IS INCEST. The father, paternal or maternal uncles, siblings, or someone or the other threatens children at home and has a sexual relationship with them. Asra was a child. The difference between a lusty touch and an affectionate parental touch can be explained. One can also explain to a girl how to recognize different touches, and how to scream, run and protect herself by telling others about it. The psychologist, Anjali, looked at Asra with astonishment. Asra looked like a person who had lost everything in a tsunami and remained detached, staring like a living corpse.

The previous day, Dr Anjali had talked to sixteen-year-old Radha, who had given birth to a child as a result of sexual abuse by her father. Radha's mother, Alivelu lost her mind because of this, and Alivelu's husband, Narasimha, had got drunk and forced his daughter, in Barkatpura.

Dr Anjali trembled thinking about Radha, who asked her repeatedly, 'Tell me doctor, you tell me, should my child call my father grandfather or father?' She told Sameena, who held Asra's hands, 'Not psychiatric treatment, her father should be given capital punishment. Probably such crimes will even increase if this is considered to be a psychological ailment. I don't think he did this due to a psychological ailment. It will take a long time to heal this child's wounds.'

'What do you want to become in the future?' Anjali asked Asra affectionately. Hope shone in Asra's eyes like a star on a new moon night, 'I'll study hard, I'll become a doctor, like you.' Sameena held Asra's hand firmly. Dr Anjali repeated, 'Counselling and psychotherapy are compulsory for ten days. She should be motivated to trust human relations.'

AMEED BROUGHT KHADRI home on bail. Khadri kept saying, 'I'm innocent' as long as he was in jail. Hafeeza and Ameed supplied biryani and beedis to him daily. As Khadri was coming out of the jail, the leader of a women's organization rushed towards him and hit his face with her slipper. The police pulled her back, saying, 'That's not correct madam, don't do that. We are there, aren't we?' Someone said, 'Asra looks exactly like her Abba.'

KHADRI WAS ALL RIGHT for four or five days. He was all right for a week or ten days. He did not say a word to Khurshid Begum. He did not raise his hand. Everyone thought he had changed. Khurshid Begum did not let him come near her. She warned him, 'Khabardar (be careful) if you touch me,' and spat on him. Khadri was all right for a month. No commotion at home. He was with Hafeeza. But…

One night, Khadri was dragging the fourteen-year-old

Shabana, Hafeeza's eldest daughter, who was sleeping next to her mother, towards the kitchen. Shabana felt as if she was falling into an abyss and screamed. Everyone woke up and understood what was happening. He threatened them with his left hand and dragged Shabana by her leg with his right hand, like a wolf. Ruksana's blood boiled. How many times had she seen him drag Asra Apa like that! She used to shiver thinking that it would be her turn next. Now that had happened, he was doing the same thing. That's it, she ran to pick up the pestle and pounced on him. She started to beat him up. He collapsed with pain. Khurshid Begum shouted, 'Beat him, beat him more, kill this demon,' and held his legs tight. Blood was streaming from Khadri's head. Ruksana beat him once more on his head with a stone lying nearby. Khadri's head broke into two – he collapsed – he did not get up again.

(Dedicated to Asra)

§

six

The Husband Stitch

'I'LL RETURN YOUR MONEY even if I've to sell my gold, Pinni (auntie), please give me money this time,' Suseela pleaded.

'Why do you want twenty thousand rupees? What do you need? Anyway, your husband gives you money every month, doesn't he?' Annapurna questioned.

'I can hardly manage with that money, Pinni, and I save nothing. The children keep asking for things. I can't refuse, nor can I buy what they want. I feel very sad. The children are not close enough to their father to ask him directly. Moreover, when is he at home? Most of the time he is with his first wife. She too has two male children,' Suseela's voice choked. She paused to control herself. 'That's why I thought of doing something,' she muttered.

'What can you do, my dear? Despite our warnings, you married that already-married fellow in the name of love. Now you are suffering,' Annapurna sounded distressed.

'I'll sell saris, Pinni, from home. I heard that saris cost much less in Surat,' Suseela put in quickly and kept looking at Pinni's face, holding her breath. Annapurna was stirring the curry. She frowned and slipped into deep thought. When she turned back, Suseela was looking at her eagerly. There were tears in Suseela's eyes; her face and nose had turned red.

Annapurna had come to a decision. 'Come around this time tomorrow. I'll manage somehow. I'll ask your Babai (uncle) for some money. But I don't know how many saris you can get for twenty thousand rupees and what kind of business you will do,' Annapurna stirred the curry once again and turned off the stove.

'You know my friend Manjula, don't you? She was my classmate in Intermediate. Now she is a government teacher. I'm planning to ask her. She will certainly give me some money,' Suseela said softly.

'Ok then, come and eat,' said Annapurna setting the plate for Suseela.

'When did you come, Suseela? I missed the bus, that's why I'm late,' said Manjula as she opened the gate. Suseela was sitting on the veranda, chatting with Manjula's mother and having tea.

'It's been almost half an hour. Go and freshen up first,' said Suseela to Manjula, who slid into the sofa, tired. Manjula's mother went in, saying, 'I'll get tea for you.'

Manjula went in, freshened up and came out to the veranda. Suseela was in a pensive mood.

'What are you thinking about, tell me? You said you were coming on some important work. What is it? Are your husband and children fine?' Manjula asked.

'Everyone is fine. I'm the only one who isn't well.' Suseela's voice was feeble.

'Why? What has happened to you now?' Manjula knew about Suseela's domestic situation and her husband, Sankarrao.

'I need thirty thousand rupees, will you give me the money?' asked Suseela without answering Manjula's question.

'What has happened, my dear? What's the matter?' Manjula insisted. In response, Suseela hid her face in her palms and started to cry. Manjula got panicky, got up and went up to Suseela and held her close. Manjula allowed her to cry for some time and then asked, 'Tell me Suseela, why do you need that much money? Do you have to pay school fees for the children? Why are you crying?'

'No, I have to have an operation,' said Suseela.

'Operation? What has happened to you?' Manjula was anxious. Suseela remained silent.

'Why don't you speak my dear, what operation?' Manjula repeated. Suseela kept quiet. Although Manjula was very affectionate and a childhood friend, and Suseela was quite free with her, she hesitated to share her problem. She was about to speak, but stopped. Her face was turning red and her lips were trembling. Manjula looked at her curiously.

What was she hiding? Wasn't Suseela's life an open book to her, Manjula wondered. She hoped Suseela did not have some dreadful disease like cancer. She questioned Suseela again.

Suseela said with difficulty, 'He is not coming to me.'

'What?' Manjula was surprised. 'Isn't your elder sister's house in your neighbourhood? Isn't he staying with both of you?' she asked.

'He does come to take care of everything. But there has been no physical relationship between us for the past one year,' Suseela was uttering each word with an effort.

'Why?' Manjula was surprised.

'He says sex with me is not good. He tells me that I've become loose and so he doesn't feel like coming to me. He goes to Akka (elder sister) always.' She wiped her tears. Manjula could understand her pain and asked her what she was planning to do.

'He should come to me again. To make that happen, I have to get operated and become as I was before marriage,' said Suseela.

'Like before marriage means…what operation are you going to have?'

'You won't understand. He says I have become loose. I'll get my vagina stitched and make it tight,' Suseela was speaking in a low voice, as if she was telling her a secret that Manjula's mother shouldn't hear. Her eyes were still moist.

Manjula was aghast. 'What? Are there such operations?' she almost yelled. 'You first tell me if you are taking the tablets for your blood pressure?' she shook Suseela by her shoulders.

SUSEELA LOOKED AT THE house opposite while unlocking her door. A Honda car was parked in front of Vijayakka's house. That meant he was there. She went in wondering if he would visit her at least that day.

Suddenly she felt weak. She lay down on the cot and curled up. She felt dizzy. She remembered that she had not taken the tablets for blood pressure that day or the previous day. She got up slowly, took the tablets and lay down on the cot again. For some reason, there was an upsurge of grief within her. She cried to her heart's content, hugging the pillow. What kind of problem was this? Was it only she who had such a problem? He used to be so nice. He was always after her during the first four years of their marriage. She knew that he was already married, but she had a mad crush on him. She ran away with him and married him in a temple. Her parents kicked her out. His first wife Vijaya attempted suicide but survived. She has two sons. Suseela has twin daughters.

He still provided everything for the home and the children. But he had gradually reduced his visits to Suseela in the past one year. The trend increased after Vijayakka gave birth to two male children, one after the other, two years after Suseela married Sankarrao.

After repeated questioning from Suseela, he said that sex life with her was not satisfactory; that she had become loose. What is this becoming loose? Is it only she who has this problem? Why doesn't Vijayakka have this problem? What should she do? She didn't know what to do even after contemplating over a long time. Her neighbour Sumathi noticed what was going on and asked, 'How is it Suseela dear that these days your husband goes only to Vijaya and does not come to you?' Suseela shed all shame and told her the reason. Sumathi asked, 'Didn't the doctor tell you Suseela, for an extra knot when she was suturing after the delivery?'

Suseela recalled that her mother had not come for her first delivery. Her maternal aunt took pity on her and took Suseela to her place for a few days. She delivered in their house. The midwife came. But Suseela did not know what she did and how she did it. She was in a semi-conscious state. When she opened her eyes, she was in a hospital in the city. She was given blood because of massive bleeding. By then there were sutures there. The lady doctor scolded Suseela, 'There are many tears inside, why did you go out of town at the time of delivery?'

Suseela asked, 'What is an extra knot?'

Sumathi looked at her sympathetically and said, 'Doesn't the vagina become wider after delivery? One extra knot is made so that it becomes tight and nice for the husband during sex. I got it done after both the deliveries. I knew about it, so I asked the doctor in advance. Of course, she asked for extra money. But, is money more important than our family life? My husband made a fuss but paid the doctor what she asked for. You should also have got it done.'

Suseela listened to her agape. Extra knot, husband stich – what were these? Pity she didn't know about these things – she felt dejected.

93

Suseela visited the doctor on Sumathi's advice. Frail women with huge bellies were sitting with fear writ large over their faces. Such a pity, would their condition also become like hers after delivery? They might get an extra stitch like Sumathi. She was not smart enough at that time, but she felt like telling the pregnant woman sitting next to her to get the extra knot after the delivery. Not just her, Suseela felt like telling all the other women sitting there. There were some women who, like her, were not pregnant. She didn't know what they were suffering from. They must have come with problems like hers – white discharge or something else. They must definitely have got it from their husbands. Women would never have any problem if their husbands behaved well. Why did women have to face these problems, Suseela wondered as she surveyed all the women waiting there. Meanwhile, her turn came.

'My husband should come to me, madam. I'll go crazy if he doesn't come to me. It's not for sex, madam. I love him. The children ask for their father. Why should he come to me madam, if I am not attractive? I want an extra knot. I delivered in a village; a midwife and not a doctor did the delivery. That's why it became loose. I want to make it tight,' Suseela went on talking.

Doctor Padmaja listened to her in amazement and explained to the doctor sitting next to her, probably because she did not understand Suseela's language, that Suseela wanted the 'husband stitch', that is, vaginoplasty.

The doctor told Suseela, 'Look, the vaginal muscles

contract after the delivery. They can enlarge and contract. In very few cases where the women have delivered ten to twelve children and have got the delivery done by midwives in villages, this problem occurs. In any case, I will examine you. Lie down.'

Suseela lay down on the examination table. The doctor examined her and said, rather surprised, 'You don't have a problem. If you want, you can bring your husband to me for counselling. I'll explain to him and tell him not to torture you like this. I'll teach you some exercises. If you do those, it will become tighter.' Padmaja tried to convince Suseela by saying, 'Anyway women have to bear all kinds of cuts and scars in the name of sutures, caesareans, hysterectomies, tubectomies and recanalizations. Is it necessary for you to cut up your body for a meaningless thing, just to satisfy your husband? Instead, do what I suggested.'

Suseela shook her head as if she were bearing intolerable pain and said with certainty, 'He won't come madam, he won't come.' With folded hands, she entreated the doctor and said with tears in her eyes, 'Madam, I want the extra knot. You must protect my family. Please tell me how much it costs.'

Doctor Padmaja had a mixed feeling of disgust and pity. 'I'll have to do it along with another surgeon. It may not be entirely successful. It will cost thirty thousand rupees. Please think about it.' Suseela was taken aback, but she recovered quickly and said, 'I'll come, madam. Somehow I will borrow the money.' While getting up to leave, she suddenly felt giddy. The nurse made her lie down on the table.

'I've high blood pressure, doctor; I am used to this. I didn't take the tablet today,' said Suseela feebly.

Her blood pressure was 160/100. Doctor Padmaja asked in surprise, 'Why do you have such high blood pressure at such a young age?'

'It's two years since the blood pressure started rising, doctor. These worries too have been increasing, you know.'

'Look Suseela, do you have to worry so much about this operation? What will you do if the blood pressure increases and leads to a heart attack or paralysis? It is more important to treat the blood pressure than this.' Padmaja warned Suseela not to stop the tablet even for a day, made the nurse give her the tablet and went on her rounds. She came back after half an hour and said, 'I've to do it when you have taken such a firm decision. But don't think that everything will be all right after the operation. Your husband might feel good. But the sutures could become too tight, sex could become painful, and you might be frightened of sex. There could be vaginal bleeding and infections. Why take a risk? Think about it once again.'

From then on Suseela started on a hunt for loans. Pinni might give her the money; hope she does. Manjula would give. She wished she had known about the extra knot before delivery. Suseela turned restlessly in the bed.

SUSEELA WAS IN THE hospital ward. It had been two hours since the operation. She regained consciousness. There was no one except Manjula by her side. Suseela had dropped her two children at her Pinni's house requesting her to look after the children for two days as she was going to Surat to buy saris for her business.

She thought the timely help from Pinni and Manjula had set things right.

'Looking at you, I'm happy that I haven't got married.' Manjula was angry, 'How many times did I tell you not to depend on that fellow but work somewhere.'

Tears welled up in Suseela's eyes, 'You won't get a husband like mine, my dear,' she said.

Suseela was happy. After the operation, the extra knot gave her courage and confidence for the future. She did not tell her husband about the extra stitch. There was bleeding from the stitches for many days, just as the doctor had warned. She went twice for check-ups.

Suseela's husband Sankarrao came to her one month after the operation. His first wife Vijaya had gone to visit her parents for a week.

Suseela went through hell that night. Unable to bear the pain and unable to scream, she endured the pain in tears, biting her lips. Although she developed a mortal fear of sex after that, she bore it for her husband's sake. She felt it was good enough that her husband was in front of her eyes. Although she bled after sex, she endured the pain. There was white discharge after that and burning during urination. Sankarrao was visiting her like he used to. That's what she wanted. Her happiness knew no bounds when she saw the children playing around Sankarrao. She wondered whether it was due to Vijayakka's absence or the effect of the extra knot. But she swam in a sea of joy. Sankarrao too looked satisfied.

Vijaya returned after a week. But Sankarrao continued to visit Suseela. He visited her only three days in a week, but Suseela was joyous. She wished to protect their bond despite the pain.

Three months went by.

Then one night Sankarrao said, 'What is this? You have come back to the same point. You have become loose again, che,' and turned away from her. Again, Sankarrao's visits became infrequent. A month or two passed by. Fear engulfed Suseela's heart. She rushed to Padmaja, frightened. Padmaja examined Suseela and said, 'It is the same, no change. Didn't I tell you that this operation may not be entirely successful! Bring your husband. I'll talk to him.'

Suseela fell back weakly on the table. Her blood pressure was 200/120. Padmaja shouted, 'Sister, Depin capsule, sublingual.' Meanwhile, Suseela collapsed.

SUSEELA WAS LYING ON the hospital bed. Her right hand was paralysed. It was hanging loose like a piece of cloth from her shoulder. Her mouth was slightly tilted to one side. She was crying. Suseela's parents, children, Annapurna Pinni, Babai were all around her. Only Manjula was standing outside the room. Thirty-year-old Manjula was wondering whether or not to accept the marriage proposal she had got recently.

§

seven

Frigid

M Y HANDS STIFFENED LIKE STICKS and tightly clasped the cot and the bed sheet. My frozen feet sunk deep into the mattress. My forehead was aching. My whole body became a weapon of resistance, tossing my head from side to side. He bent over me hungrily, holding my head forcibly and biting my lips. His saliva was on my lips. Idiot, doesn't clean his teeth properly. How many times had he slapped me for telling him to brush thoroughly! Rogue. My stomach was churning at the stench from his mouth. He inflicted the stinking atrocity on my lips for five minutes and abused me for resisting him. Is this romance? Like kneading dough, his hands were squeezing my breasts madly with all their strength. I was suffocating with pain. Unaffected, he kept biting me hard, and silenced my wailing with his threats.

How shall I bear this violence? The more I froze, the more he groaned and attacked me like a bear. He cooled down after a while, pushed my knees away with a half-satisfied look and said, 'You're frigid, didn't your mother tell you how to make your husband happy? You stiffen like a stick!' Obnoxious blabber.

The very next minute he was in the ecstasy of sleep, snoring, unaware of the damage caused by his ravaging on my body. How could he sleep so peacefully? I was in shock like a field of green crops wrecked by a herd of stamping buffaloes. There was an unbearable stench emanating from my body. I rushed into the bathroom and poured water over my unclean body. My tears were uncontrollable. Is this romance – pain for me and pleasure for that fellow? Is this romance – to attack, pinch, bite, scratch the woman's body and finally leave saliva or semen on her? Does it have nothing to do with a woman's feelings, responses, pain, suffering, likes, dislikes? I read somewhere that romance does not mean mere friction between the male and female genital organs. It's a beautiful body language in which the couple expresses love through sincere touch with affection, responsibility and respect. But I have never experienced this. In the past two-and-a-half years, in these daily physical wars that take place in this bedroom, amidst the saga of atrocities, many refusals, many more helpless tears and struggles, he has been the winner, and the loser too.

He has always been unconcerned about my likes, dislikes, pain, disgust, desire. Was it even possible for me to burn with passion for this fellow? I am reminded of a lusty dog in heat when I see him. No sensitive feeling, love or empathy.

On an evening or a pleasant moonlit night, amidst the flowers and aroma of love, a garland of smiles along with a garland of jasmines! A warm impression of his lips on my neck, my face in his cupped hands and an endearing signature of fragrances on my lips! If only I could hear him whisper my name, Kasturi, into my ears! The trance of desire that starts in a stream and floods us away, the longing of love expressed in sensitive body language, a rapturous journey of bodies, a celebration of union that is manifested only when the two hearts unite...all this is mere romanticism. In him, the fragrance of romance was nothing but the stench of his mouth or the mixed odour of whisky and cigarettes. He whispered only abuses into my ears. Body language meant his breaking my joints. That's all. Where was the romance? It was a mere hair-raising experience.

He lay beside me, snoring. The fellow knew no tender touch, but only beastly lust. I lay beside him. How strange it was to have to sleep next to the person who committed sexual atrocities and violence on me every day! Yes, because what he did is licensed atrocity in the name of marriage. Marital rapes within four walls of home have societal acceptance. It is the man's right. Who wrote this? Whenever I think of running back home, I am reminded of my mother crying helplessly. I am a prisoner; I cannot go anywhere.

It is dawn already. The milk boy is ringing the bell. I have to get up. Housework, then work in office throughout the day, and housework again in the evening. At night, there is the daily physical activity of the fellow whether I like it or not and whether I had the patience or not. The experiments he conducted with my body have led to sleepless nights with pain and humiliation. But I have to get up. I have to get up in the morning – have to fill water for drinking, boil milk and serve tea to him, have to supply him everything from his toothbrush to his shoes. The only thing the idiot does is clean himself after relieving himself in the toilet. I have to finish cooking in a hurry, pack lunch boxes and fill water bottles, serve him patiently, gulp down some food and start the drama of travel on the city bus.

'Can't understand atrocity on a sixty-year-old woman,' his loud comment while reading the newspaper. Probably he meant that sexual atrocity should be perpetrated only on young women. Isn't what you do with me every night sexual atrocity, you fellow? But then it carries the dirty label of conjugality, I thought vengefully and went into the kitchen.

Some old friend of his came on a visit. Greetings, surprises, pleasantries. He said, 'I couldn't come for your wedding Kameswarrao, how is your married life?' My husband, Kameswarrao, he is *kamam* (lust) all over. He giggled saying it was good and shouted, 'Kasturi, get coffee.' What happy married life? Awful married life! Happy, for whom? This is not marriage, you fellow, this is desecration of my body, heart, life, everything.

The friend left. Kameswarrao screamed like hungry cattle in a shed. There was not an iota of regret on this beast's face during the day, though he occupied my body by force and poked my body and mind at night. As if all that happened was natural, he made me do the housework like a slave and ate his fill.

One day, there was a scar on my cheek, where he had bitten me the previous night. I was worried about going to office with that bite mark. He said irritably, 'Apply some medicine and lighten it fast.' To add fuel to fire, the neighbourhood aunt said, 'Oh, your husband is very romantic, Kasturi.' She said it like a cheap joke in a third-rate Telugu movie, within his earshot. That woman thought she was flirting. What a glow of satisfaction on his face! Disgusting! You, mad woman, I was almost dead when he bit me. I should have taken a video of the rape scene between us and shown it to you. Why couldn't you say, 'Oh my dear, it has become red. Is it painful? How could your husband behave like a beast?'

Such a comment would only intensify the violent insanity in him! He might turn more aggressive that night. If I too bit him sharply like that in love, wouldn't he scream like me? What if I scared him by closing his mouth like he did with me? Couldn't I also pinch his thigh to prevent him from screaming? How would he go to office the next day with scars on his face? But did I have the capacity to do that? Before I could do something like that, I would be lying dead in a corner with his blows. No way.

It seems that in some country, wives show each other bleeding wounds and marks as evidence of their husbands' romance the next morning. One day, he showed me this piece of news in a sex column, proudly. I saw the dark shadows of those wounds and tears on those women's faces. That fellow, the sexologist was a man. How else would you expect him to write? The intensity of the wound is a measure of the man's romance, it seems, as if it does not matter even if the woman dies in the process. They did not call it sadism, a kind of sexual problem and psychological illness that needed treatment.

How many times had I told my mother that I could no longer bear the violence and that I wished to return to her. But she did not agree. 'Please adjust, my dear,' she said. It seems she too adjusted with my father. Father...! Was he too like this Kameswarrao with my dear mother? Father, who shed tears when he saw me off to my in-laws' house. Father, who scolded the teacher for beating me up in school...was he like Kameswarrao with my mother? Why like? Wasn't he the same?

What about my elder brother...the brother who rejoiced in my tying a *rakhi* around his wrist? Sometimes my sister-in-law looked anxious. Once when I barged into her room, she hooked up her blouse in a hurry, but I had seen the Burnol-smeared scars on her delicate bosom. The tube of Burnol came under my feet, and all the ointment oozed out.

Father, brother – are you really what you are? Is this really true? No, no, if you remove the masks, the demons will appear. Kameswarrao too is a good, gold-like brother to his younger sister.

Women amidst crowds, with handbags and water bottles hanging from their shoulders, are waiting for the bus in the hot sun, sweating. The pain and anxiety at missing the bus are writ on the faces of the panting women. Venkatalakshmi, who carries lunch box every day, shouts at a driver who does not stop his bus, 'You bloody fellow, stop the bus, what will you lose?' She is gasping for breath and snapping her fingers. Working women, waiting for the bus, are anxious and irritated because the bus does not come. How distressed they must be at home day and night! Their hearts must be crushed with the naggings of their mothers-in-law and sisters-in-law. Like me, they cool down their bodies, inflamed by their husbands' demonic sex, with cold water in the morning, hide their bodies in the layers of rough cotton saris, smear some face powder or turmeric powder on their downcast, shadowed faces, put on some sprightliness, immerse themselves in their work, try to forget their sorrows. The delay in the arrival of the bus increases their irritation. Is that all? Is that all to life?

But does everyone have a husband like Kameswarrao? My childhood friend Srujana's husband Madhusudan is very good, it seems. He helps her with the housework. He fondly calls her Suji. If on a particular day she says, 'No please, I am not in the mood,' or complains of pain, he does not even touch her. He says, 'No problem,' holds her close, presses her head to his chest and sleeps hugging her firmly. Wish my husband were like him. He makes me slog throughout the day, growling all the time. At night, he harasses me for sex as if he owns me. Che…

Why doesn't this wretched bus come…

'WHY ARE YOU LATE? Didn't get the bus again? I will get you the loan, why don't you buy a scooter? Why this race ruining your health, instead of cooking tasty food, eating happily, sleeping comfortably, nurturing the body and giving pleasure to your husband?' The useless chatter of our boss, who kills us every day with his filthy looks.

The bus comes finally. Pushing and getting pushed, I am somehow propelled into the bus along with others. No space to even move one's legs. To add to the woes, a few lecherous men take advantage of the situation to touch women's bodies and feast with their hungry gazes, with no regard for the women's discomfiture. Don't these fellows with multiple faces know that their wives, daughters and mothers too were squeezed by other men in buses, were insulted every day by male insects like them and that they broke down when they reached home, hiding their heads in their mother's bosom or pillows?

As I was entering the office one morning, I heard the cashier Sudheer asking Ramani with a sneer, 'Ramani, you spent a long time in the boss' room. What is the story?' Ramani said, 'Shut up.' Her eyes were red. It seems that the boss had pressed Ramani's hands while handing her the file and said, 'What have you decided Ramani? I pity you. I'll keep you with me all my life. I will buy you a flat. Tell me, will you live with me?' He had got up quickly and pulled her onto his lap. Ramani had slapped him angrily and come away, with her heart burning like a ball of fire. The suspicious neighs of the beast Sudheer outside! The boss who had been slapped by her was screaming from inside, 'You are past thirty-two. You are not getting married. You are getting old and stale. How dare you slap me for offering to keep you.' My heart burnt. It was good that Ramani had slapped him. Why did the mean fellow desire to have Ramani as his keep? He had a good wife, children who were studying in intermediate, own house, a comfortable bank balance, a car and a secure life. Why did he have the dirty desire to raise his status by having a second set-up? He had been harassing women. Last year, when he harassed a girl called Parimala, she left the job and went away.

'Probably I'll lose my job. But you know how he hugged me close to his body? In that one second, imagine how many places he touched greedily! Che, dog! I've finally done a good thing by slapping him,' Ramani was panting. She ran towards the sink red-faced, 'I'll go home and take a bath. Che, let me at least wash my hands.'

Thirty-two-year-old Ramani was a postgraduate, good-looking. But she was not married yet. She said she did not want to, that's all. She did not give any reasons. Ramani's mother had urged me to ask Ramani as to when she would marry, and in response she said, 'You are married, how happy are you Kasturi? Don't I see you every day? My elder sister and her beautiful life were destroyed when she married my beast-like brother-in-law. Unable to tolerate his waywardness, my sister hanged herself. I have lost faith in the system of marriage after seeing you and my elder sister. I have no interest in marriage. I will carry on like this. In any case, how does it matter to me! I can easily fix these dog-like bosses! Probably he will put a black mark on my service record. Probably he will remove me from service; let him do so. One of my friends is running a mahila sangham (women's group). I will complain there. This fellow will realize what I am and the power of a woman when my friend comes to this office for an inquiry. Take care of your work. What is that scar on your face? Did he beat you again? How long will you put up with that sadist husband? Why don't you file a domestic violence case? Is he torturing you for dowry and a car?' Ramani tried to prod me.

Buses are usually crowded in the evening as most offices close around that time. Ramani and I managed to get seats in the front row. College girls were standing even on the footboard and chatting. It was so crowded that no one could bother about others. A man of around thirty-five, in a white shirt and pants was standing behind the two college girls. The fellow was deliberately leaning on one of the girls. She was struggling to prevent his contact, bending forward as far as she could. I wish she would turn back and kick him boldly. Ramani was chatting. I was listening to Ramani, but my attention turned again towards the girls, and I was shocked. I was horrified, my heart cringed with abhorrence, and my body trembled with rage at what the rogue was doing. He had unzipped his pants and was rubbing his organ against her back.

My seat was in line with him, and so it was clearly visible to me. His face reddened with lust, and there were red streaks in his eyes. I didn't know what to do. I lost my voice with anger. Then I spotted the conductor in front of me. I didn't know what I said screaming while pointing towards them.

The conductor looked in the direction and froze, not knowing what to do. Then he yelled to stop the bus, pounced on the man abusing, 'You bastard, son of a dog,' and pushed him by the collar from the bus, which still had not come to a halt. The fellow had not zipped up completely. He went away somewhere, crawling like a dog on the road. But meanwhile, he had done whatever he had wanted to. The manifestation of his lust was flowing like starch down the back of the girl in a brown churidar. She turned back at the commotion, was shocked, and repeatedly bent and looked at her back with anger, distress, insult and hatred, unable to wipe the dirt away and at the same time unable to carry it on her body.

That girl who was not even sixteen, got down from the bus, jumped into an auto and vanished, wailing. The silence of a graveyard descended upon the bus. Ramani was dumbfounded. Many others were in a similar state. I was reminded of my paternal uncle and the grandfather who gave tuitions. My heart shuddered. The bus jumped forward with a jolt with the conductor's whistle and his scream, 'Where do these bastards come from? Right, right.'

When would that girl's wound heal?

My forehead was splitting with pain. What a dreadful past I had? How could I forget the devastation that my paternal uncle wreaked in my life? That wound was still aching raw. The fear and hatred that I saw on the face of that sixteen-year-old on the bus was something I had experienced eighteen years ago. How despicable he was! Exactly like my uncle. He was my own uncle, shared my father's blood. He destroyed my

109

life. Mother and father would always be busy. Father was into business and mother was a Central government employee. Both of them would leave in the morning and return between six and seven in the evening. Father would immediately leave for the club and mother would get immersed in housework.

I was thirteen and in the eighth class when he landed in my house from another town to study computer science. He looked much like my father. But his behaviour was strange. He would look awkwardly at my growing breasts and my legs below the skirt. He would wink at me. When my parents were absent, he would show me obscene pictures on the internet. When I told mother, she said, 'Che, keep quiet, father would kill if he came to know.' Who would he kill, me? Why? Wouldn't he kill uncle? Would he kill me? Why? What did I do? Wasn't it uncle who was doing wrong? It was all very confusing. Who should I tell?

I attained puberty the same year. I still remember the waves of fear that the warm blood flowing down my legs created in me. When I asked, 'Mother, where does the blood come from?' my mother said, 'Che, why do you have to know about it? All girls go through this,' looking around to see if someone was listening. I did not obey my mother when she asked me to give something to uncle or to serve him food. His gaze was always stuck to my body and stopped me from going close to him. He would hit my breasts with his elbow while crossing me and say sorry as if he had done it by mistake. He would barge into my room while I was changing and stare at my body greedily and then say sorry as if he had done it unknowingly. Days passed in fear of uncle's disgusting acts, the uncle who shared my father's blood. Uncle's eyes would loiter around the window of my room at midnight. I used to die with fear.

My room was next to my parents' room. 'Please leave me, I'm tired. Tomorrow, okay? Today is the third day of my periods. I've a stomach ache. I plead with you. Last time the pain and bleeding increased. Please leave me,' mother's helpless voice. 'Shh, keep quiet. You keep grumbling every day. All pretexts. Didn't Dr Bhramaram say that one can have sex during periods and that nothing will happen? All pretexts. Why have you lost interest in me? Have you found a paramour in the office? Should I go to prostitutes? Turn this way, won't you?' I could hear the sound of blows on my mother's back. The sounds of grief that my mother suppressed by stuffing the pallu of her sari into her mouth broke into fragments and reached me even though I didn't want to hear. I could understand but also could not understand that father was doing something to mother...unable to see all that I would run into my room, scared. I wouldn't have gone to see had I not heard my mother's wailing. Why was father doing that? I hated it. How could I love my father if he tortured my mother?

If ever I stood at the threshold and talked to the neighbourhood girls and boys, my father would say, 'What are you doing there like a prostitute bitch? Come in.' How could he say that, call his own daughter a prostitute bitch? I would cringe. 'What? Why is your blouse so tight and revealing? Go and change, you bitch,' he shouted, and I ran inside, scared. Why couldn't he say softly, 'Your dress is not okay Kasturi, wear slightly loose clothes, my dear'? Should he suffix every sentence with the word 'bitch'? I wailed wondering if my name were bitch or Kasturi.

I used to hope that mother would not speak to him in the morning and would angrily question him after weeping the entire night. Instead, father would say, 'Rajani, give me this or give me that. Give me a cup of coffee. Have you paid Kasturi's fees? Didn't I ask you to come here?' Mother would say pleasantly, 'I have paid, wait please, take this tea,' smiling. I would be shocked. How was it possible?As if all that happened at night was natural, something to do with only the night, and the day had nothing to do with it.

I stopped talking to my father for calling me a prostitute bitch. I asked my mother how he could say such a thing to his daughter and asked her to question him. But she overlooked everything, including the blows she got. I used to get angry with her though she was older than me in age, when she talked to him with a smile.

Sometimes mother would have teeth marks on her cheeks and lips. She was fair. She would hold the pallu of her sari between her teeth and wear her blouse. That is when I would see red marks on her beautiful bosom. When I enquired, she would say that they were scratches from a plant or that the seasoning fell on her, panicking a little. I saw tears in her eyes several times. I knew that father had done something to her. Was it only father, or were all men like that? Our neighbour,

Sudhakar uncle, Vinay uncle who lived in the house opposite, maternal uncles, grandfathers, science teacher – were all of them like that with their wives? Are all men like that? I developed a dislike for father, and it began to grow. Was my brother also going to be the same when he grew up?

MEANWHILE, UNCLE'S NASTY behaviour started to become worse. One day, mother and father went to attend a wedding, promising to come back by ten in the night. I had a fever and I was sleeping. Mother wanted to stay with me, but father did not allow her to do so as my paternal grandmother would be angry if my mother skipped the function. Uncle left that morning, saying that he was going back to his place. He appeared without warning at around seven in the evening. As I was alone at home he pounced on me like a wild animal. He increased the volume of the TV.

I cried helplessly, pathetically and pleaded with him, 'Uncle, please leave me, don't do anything to me, I fall at your feet.' I didn't know where to run, so I hid under the cot, frightened. How the fellow came searching for me! Completely naked, red eyes, hair all over the body, something protruding horribly between the legs – like a three-legged human beast he pulled me by my legs from under the cot. He held my hair, tossed me on the cot, fell brutally on me, pulled off my clothes, squeezed and bit my breasts. Pain, as if a sharp knife had been plunged between my thighs. He hushed my screams with his hand on my mouth. I was wriggling like a chick with its neck severed, crying. He threatened me, his finger raised, 'I'll kill you if you let your mother and father know about this.' I was resisting and sobbing, but before they reached, he fell on me once again and satisfied his demonic lust. I woke up in the hospital. Severe bleeding. It seems the vagina had a deep cut. Doctors' questions...some asking how he did it and others asking how many times he did it and still others asking how many tears there were in the vagina. Questions and more questions. Humiliated and wounded, I yelled at all of them to leave. I felt like dying. Severe pain for fifteen days. Unable to get off the bed and move, excruciating burning while urinating, I was afraid of urinating. I could walk slowly only after a month. The entire colony came to know about it. Uncle fled from our house.

Mother became almost mad. She made me promise that I wouldn't tell anyone about it. When people talked about lodging a police complaint and approaching women's organizations, she wept saying that we would be dishonoured and that the girl wouldn't get married. Father became almost silent. There was a rage in me. I thought that if I saw uncle, I would kill him. First I would sever the third leg between his two legs. I would scream madly that I would kill uncle. I would hug my mother and sleep at night. I was scared of darkness and of being alone at home. I didn't allow father to come close to me either. What if he were also like uncle... Hadn't I seen him falling on mother and squeezing her, even though she cried and objected? When father tried to draw me close to him lovingly, I shoved him off and ran away. He cried. Several times, with his head in mother's lap, he sobbed,

'We should have listened to her, Rajani. When she told us about that wretched fellow, we hushed her up saying uncle is not that kind and went to our offices. We should have stopped for a minute and listened to her. We spent too much time in offices and clubs.' Father cried, beating his head. In fact, I had asked them to stay back instead of attending the wedding that day. Mother had said, 'You should be brave as you are growing up.' Hadn't I said that uncle was behaving like that because I was growing up, he might come when you are not around, no, please don't go? My mother had said, 'Che, uncle is not in town. Moreover, open the door only if I call you, ok?' She went away, and uncle came like the dubious jackal, and left after devouring me.

Mother and father changed a lot after that. Father spent almost the whole time at home in the evening. Both of them applied for two months' leave. They pleaded with me and made me take some tablets. I took them and slept drowsily. I couldn't write the examinations that year. Mother crumbled when people showed sympathy. Brother, who was a year older than me, cried saying, 'What happened to my sister?' At least he should not behave like uncle when he grows up. How could I tell him what happened to me and why uncle fell on me and beat me so hard between the legs to make me bleed profusely though I was crying as though I were going to die. Some TV channels and newspapers discussed everything and showed my photograph. Mother wept, beating her head. I too wept. When Kalpana Chawla's photograph had been published in newspapers for flying in space, I longed

115

for my photograph to be published in newspapers. I knew my photograph would be published if I achieved something great like Kalpana Chawla, so I decided to do something significant. But my photograph was published for something very different. Father got himself transferred to some other district.

Gradually I recovered. The injury caused by uncle had not healed. I started going to school, but did not talk or play with boys. I was haunted by fear. I did not talk to male teachers either. In due course, I completed my postgraduation. In the meantime, I received one or two proposals, but I refused to get married. I was taken to a counsellor. He said that all men were not like that and advised me to get married. But my hatred for men and romance did not go away. My fear about life after marriage kept increasing. Suddenly father died of a heart attack. The attack was brought on by his worry about me. Before he died, he made me promise that I would get married. Then mother was left all alone. I finally married Kameswarrao as I had given my word to my father. That he was a psychopath came to light only after our marriage. He was brought up by his stepmother amidst beatings and insults. He filled his entire self with hatred for her, transformed it into vengeance against all women and finally targeted me.

As it is, I was uninterested in romance. I had thought he would convince, cajole and love me like Srujana's husband Madhusudan. The very first night, he manifested his beastliness and abused me, even as I was cringing with fear and pain. 'You, frigid woman, didn't your mother teach you how to make your husband happy?' Probably his father did not teach this beast how to treat a woman with sensitivity and respect. My conjugal life with him for the past two and half years had been filled with a hundred atrocities and two hundred refusals.

I would have compromised even if this fellow were a male chauvinist and crazy. But he was a sex maniac. I was horrified even at the idea of natural sex, but this fellow did unnatural things with me and made me experience hell. I was dying because of him. Someday I'll kill him. The event in the bus brought back bitter memories of my childhood. This fellow was obsessed with obscene movies and sex sites on the internet. He used his strength on me, demanding that I imitate the people in those movies and sites. Of late, he had been collecting material on Viagra. New tablets were found in his pockets every other day. I was dying unable to face his valour even for a minute. Probably he would take viagras and bhayagras (scary devices and means) and manifest his masculinity. Starting from three-year-old girls to seventy-year-old women, everyone is becoming a scapegoat to two-three minutes of men's valour. What would happen to women if they take the viagras and keep raising it for hours like uncles and my husband, Kameswarrao? Wouldn't women turn into frigids?

Grief welled up like flood and it was drowning me. I had tried to forget the bitter childhood memories, reluctantly agreed to marriage, tried to get rid of the fear of sex and started life with a lot of hope, but every night of my conjugal life was a nightmare of atrocities. In the past two and half years, I had not got the happiness and minimum respect due in family life even on a single day. My body revolted with fear and hatred even if he placed his hand on me. At that moment, I was reminded of uncle. Let alone happiness; I had not experienced even a loving touch or a tender kiss from my husband. Like a bull rampaging through the fields and attacking viciously, he falls on my body, attacking and smothering me; gasping for breath, he leaves the semen in and on my body and turns to the other side and sleeps. Whenever possible he conducts his perverted experiments on me, and if I refuse, he calls me a bitch, accuses me of being frigid and batters me. How long should I continue to live with him without friendship, love and intimacy?

Earlier I used to ask myself can't I change this man? Probably he was like that because he was raised by not so loving stepmother. He might change. If I tried to draw close to him in a slow, loving and friendly manner, he would say the prostitute act wouldn't work with him. The crudeness broke my heart into pieces, and I remained dull, weak, rigid and frigid. I had not told this fellow why I was frigid. How he rejoiced in calling me that. I should tell him, should tell him about uncle, the boss who tortured Ramani in office, the beast that unzipped his pants and fell on the tender sixteen-year-old on the bus. I should tell him how despicable he was at night. The sixteen-year-old girl's face that turned dark with fear, hatred, insult and shock and reddened the next minute was haunting me. Probably my face too had been like that when uncle did that. My initial nights with Kameswarrao were perhaps like that. Don't these people see the dark shadows of fear and hatred on the women's faces? The rascals probably imagine that the women are blushing. How do I control this grief? How do I get rid of this horrible headache? I don't feel like cooking, don't feel like switching on the light. I leave the door ajar and sleep in the hall. I wake up with a jolt at night.

'You didn't close the door. For which paramour of yours did you keep the door open?' Kameswarrao had pulled off my sari and was enveloping me. Che che, he is drunk again. He fell on me while I was sleeping in the hall. I cannot bear the stench. My heart is like a ball of fire. I am reminded of uncle again. That helpless girl's scream in the bus, that mad male beast's perverted act in the bus – all the same. This fellow is even worse. I use my entire strength and wriggle to shove him away. 'Leave me, leave me, you bastard,' I shout. He gets a jolt and looks at me madly. 'You bitch, you call me names,' he slaps me. He is blabbering, 'You bitch, you don't agree even on one night, you frigid, f*** your mother,' and he falls on me. My rage knows no bounds. I kick him hard. He is drunk and weak, so falls to a side. I stand up quickly, kick him hard between his legs with my right leg and shout angrily, 'You beast, I'll tell you why I became frigid.' I growl like a tiger. I kick him again, again and again until his testicles split. He falls like a dog bending his legs with pain. I am overwhelmed by breathlessness and anger; I beat him to my heart's content with an umbrella. I walk into the bedroom and start to pack my suitcase. First, I should get out of here and then at least reach out to help the tender children who get wounded every day at home, outside and in buses, hug them to my bosom, wipe their tears. Ramani, in any case, would be there.

§

eight

The Swish of the Sword

THE LUB–DUB SOUND BECAME LOUDER. Amma's heartbeat became faster. That means Nanna has come and an atmosphere of terror pervaded. When he was not at home, Amma lived in fear like an innocent rabbit, not knowing when the wild animal would attack her. When he was at home, she shivered like a rabbit about to become a prey to the wild animal.

I was growing up warmly in Amma's womb. After completing the third month, I got used to hearing the frightened heartbeat that resembled the screams of birds flapping their wings, panicking at the sound of a gunshot. Amma's heartbeat echoed with fear, agony, anger, helplessness and grief. The music of her life had lost its rhythm, snuffed out by a cruel man, Nanna.

Why was Amma so scared of Nanna? In the beginning I couldn't understand, but slowly I did. Nanna was a drunkard.

Every day he got drunk and bashed up Amma. Though he knew I was in Amma's womb, he lost his senses when he battered her. He beat her if she did not arrange water for his bath or if the water was too cold or too hot. Amma had to wake up at four in the morning, and walk down the stairs to fill water from the handpump. She would make coffee and wake him up, dreading. He would open his eyes abusing her. If anything was wrong with the coffee, Amma's cheeks had to split. One day, he threw the cup of coffee at Amma saying that it did not have enough sugar. Amma tried to escape but could not. The coffee fell on her hands and burned her hands red. Her cry of distress moved me very much. Another day, he poured a bucket of water on Amma saying it was too hot, and slapped her. Amma slogged for him shivering, running, wriggling, holding her breath until Nanna left for the factory, even if she was not well.

Nanna was cruel. It seems he had been that way since childhood. Nannamma told Amma when she visited us, 'You only have to adjust Sudheera, don't make him angry. He becomes a monster if things are not to his liking or not ready on time. The first wife separated, unable to live with this fellow.' So, Amma was Nanna's second wife. The first wife suffered his cruelty for four years, got frustrated and divorced him. It has only been one and a half years since Amma married Nanna.

Amma's heartbeat doubled during the night. Nanna was not only cruel and a drunkard, but also lustful. Yes, I am Nanna's daughter saying this about my father. Amma shuddered with pain, screamed saying no, pleaded with tears in her eyes, held his feet. Nanna would not listen to her. He burnt Amma's cheeks, lips, breasts and waist with cigarettes. Amma would suppress the pain, biting her lips in silence. But how long could she do that? If she cried, Nanna abused her, twisted her hands and tortured her. At times Amma swallowed the screams that struggled to come out of her as if her blood vessels were about to burst, by squeezing the pallu of her sari in her mouth. Those waves of agony touched Amma's stomach and then travelled to me. I quivered in Amma's womb. Sometimes that lustful fellow cut Amma's hands with a blade. Amma wailed like a bleeding, lonely pigeon whose wings had been severed. I wept in Amma's womb. He found new ways of torturing her. Sometimes Amma tried to escape from him. But where could she go beyond that room and that house? That monster haunted her. He bit her tender lips so hard that they bled. He bit her cheeks, leaving teeth marks. Amma endured all the pain helplessly. I wished she would kill that fellow.

Unable to bear the pain, Amma would shudder, holding her stomach. At such times, her stomach would contract. I would feel suffocated and move up. I could feel Amma's fingers from outside and could hear Amma's sobs from inside. Amma, how can I save you?

Amma's parents were very poor. After her father had passed away, Ammamma struggled hard to bring up Amma and got her married. Ammamma's lifetime earnings were spent on Amma's marriage. They were told that Nanna's first wife had a relationship with someone else and ran away with him. That Nanna was a sadist who resorted to physical torture was concealed from them.

Ammamma's acquaintances fixed the match, it seems. Whenever Ammamma came to our house, Amma lay down with her head in Ammamma's lap and cried her heart out. I felt as if I were swimming in Amma's tears. Ammamma too was helpless. She said, 'Stop it, my child, you have to bear it,' stroking Amma's body. I would get angry. Why should she bear it? Ammamma saw the cigarette burns and the cuts on Amma's body, and she once said to him, though afraid, 'She is pregnant, don't torture her like that, my son.'

That night, Amma had to face more hellish experiences as a bonus. 'You bitch, did you tell your Amma? Why don't you call her now,' he abused her. Do you know where he burnt her that day? On her genitals. Yes, he burnt her with a cigarette on the genitals that were preparing for my birth. The room reverberated with Amma's distressed cries. Nanna closed her mouth to prevent her shrieks from being heard outside. Every day he ruthlessly used Amma's delicate body for his lust. Though he had already fallen below the level of a human being, on that day his battering reached the peak of his cruelty. I was seething. I wriggled in Amma's womb, helpless, angry, disgusted and agitated. What should I do to that fellow? Why do women helplessly endure men's atrocities? Why do men subject women to violence? Who gives them the right? Why don't women protest?

Nanna violated Amma every day and abused her

physically. Amma endured everything silently, weeping. Why? Why didn't she protest and beat him up? Why didn't she too cut him with a blade? Why didn't she too burn him with a cigarette? Probably Nanna was very strong and Amma was frail. Amma might collapse if Nanna pushed her with one hand. But then couldn't Amma stab him with a sharp weapon like a knife and save herself? No, it was not just the body that was the reason, there were other reasons as well. I was unable to understand. Questions! Questions!! Questions!!!

Someone raped a girl called Neeraja in our neighbourhood. She had gone to a movie with her friend. While she was on her way back, someone dragged her into the bushes and violated her. By the time her friend escaped and informed people, Neeraja's life was ruined. Amma went and consoled her and cried, hugging Neeraja to her bosom. I was extremely moved by their wailing. While some fellow committed sexual atrocity on Neeraja once, Amma was being violated every day by Nanna, with whom she should have been living with love and trust. How miserable! Neeraja's mother held Amma and cried saying, 'Sudheera, what will happen to my daughter's life?'

I was seven months old in Amma's womb. My attachment with Amma, her woes and her tears was increasing. Amma got the newspaper from the neighbour's house every day and read it. Like all other things, I understood the news when Amma read the newspaper. I was frightened, surprised, disgusted and agitated when I heard the news. There was some horrible news that day. A six-year-old girl was watching TV through a window. Some boys who were twelve or thirteen covered her with a cloth, took her away and raped her. She bled horribly. I felt depressed. Another day, a twelve-year-old girl called Jyothi was lured with chocolates by a fifteen-year-old boy called Sreenivas, who raped and battered her with sticks and stabbed her to death.

From six to sixty, women were being victimized by the demonic lust of male beasts. Did their lust have no regard for childhood and old age? In Britain, a drunkard fought with his wife and raped his 13-month-old child in front of her. How horrible and callous!

The rape and murder of Jayanti the other day, Ponnamma's rape and death yesterday – what's all this? Are women's bodies easily available commodities to fulfil men's shameful lust? Where did the fault lie – in men's thoughts or women's bodies? Amma was distraught reading the news. She placed her hand on her stomach and wished with all her strength, please don't be a girl. What if I were a girl child – I was frightened.

Nanna stayed back home one day and took Amma to the hospital. He wanted to get a scan done to know if I was a girl or a boy. He wanted only a male child. He would hack Amma to death if he got to know that I was a girl. Amma was trembling. That means they would know if I was a boy or a girl. My genitals would be seen on scanning. If I was a girl, would I be Amma, Neeraja, Jyothi, the six-year-old Munni who was raped and killed or the sixty-year-old Satyamma who was raped?

If I was a boy, would I become like Nanna or like the other lusty male beasts like Nanna?

Like Amma, I too became increasingly tense. My eyes were contracted all those days, so I did not know who I was. The scanning was done, and the report revealed that I was a girl. Nanna's face was flushed. Amma was sweating all over with fear. Should Amma and women like Amma have to experience such blood curdling moments for a girl child? Would the joy and grief of a being decided by gender even before one is born?

That night Nanna subjected Amma to hell again. He had demonic sex with her, with me as the witness. It felt as if not Amma alone but all the women in the world were helpless. It felt as if I, who was in Amma's womb, was being threatened. The agony in me was rising. The conflict boiling in me for months was intensifying. Why should I be born? If my identity was so horrific and my gender so damning even before I was born, what would happen after my birth? That moment I looked at myself with much effort. My genitals terrified me. Aren't these the genitals that men stab mercilessly and rape lustfully? Would I face inhuman atrocities due to these genitals? Would I have to lead a slave's life like Amma's? No, I can't bear it. I have to do something. What should I do? I must use all my energy and turn my body into a weapon to teach a lesson to these men. I must take revenge for Amma's tears and the tears of all women who were being subjected to such atrocities. I was simmering and writhing like wildfire. Amma, my decision might make your life worse, but you cannot but sacrifice. Amma, won't you forgive me?

IT WAS A PRIVATE HOSPITAL. There was commotion all over. Sudheera delivered in the hospital where she went for regular check-ups. The doctors were murmuring in astonishment. All the famous gynaecologists and scientists in the city were there, including the sonologist who confirmed after scanning that Sudheera had a girl child in her womb. They were shaking their heads in shock. What astounded them was that the child had no genitals. Instead, she had a sharp horn-like structure. The urinary passage on both sides was normal, but below that was a sharp, horn-like part. The baby was otherwise healthy. Her eyes were flashing. The satisfaction of having conquered the world reflected in her sparkling eyes.

nine

§

Murder!

'AKKA, I SUSPECT MANJEERA IS PREGNANT. She denied it when I asked her. You ask her once.' But Shyamala dismissed Kamala's suspicion, saying, 'Nothing like that. As it is, she is chubby. It looks like she has put on weight now and her stomach is looking inflated. How can she not inform me, her mother?' Though Shyamala said this, she was anxious. Manjeera visited her after one year. Of late, she had rarely been visiting her parents. She had almost stopped calling them. Whenever Shyamala called her, either the phone was switched off, or she did not answer the phone.

Manjeera came when her grandmother died. Her husband and her nine-year-old daughter, Keertana, accompanied her. They wanted to leave the same night. They refused to stay, though Shyamala pleaded with them. Both of them were looking dejected for some reason. Shyamala thought they were sad about the grandmother's demise.

'Manji, did you miss your period?' she asked.

Manjeera was shocked. Nagesh chipped in with, 'No Attayya, she doesn't have any work to do. My mother does the cooking. Manjeera simply sits and eats. Obviously she will put on weight. It's time for our bus. We will leave now, Attayya. Manji and Keertana, let's start now.'

Shyamala said, 'Nagesh, you are not allowing them to stay at least until the ceremonies are complete!' But he left, along with his wife and daughter.

SHYAMALA COULDN'T SLEEP that night. Visions of Manjeera were dancing before her eyes. It was exactly nine years since she had got married. She had become a part of a joint family, being the second daughter-in-law. Her sister-in-law, Sangeetha, had two sons by then. One was five years old and the other two. Manjeera did not conceive for two years after marriage. There was much anxiety regarding this. Nagesh was also worried because their friends and relatives who had got married around the same time all had children. Manjeera's mother-in-law started saying that she was not well and that she wanted to see Nagesh's children before she died. It was then that Manjeera's gynaecological check-ups started. She was put on hormonal treatment to facilitate the release of an egg. It was said that the problem was with her obesity and that it could be remedied by walking and yoga. Manjeera tried her best to walk and practise yoga to reduce her weight. She conceived Keertana after six months. Nagesh was happy, but expressed dissatisfaction with the fact that it was not a male child, saying that his brother had two boys. He did not stop there and went on to say that Manjeera must give birth to a male child next time, as if it were in her hands. Nagesh waited as the doctor warned him not to think of another child for two years since Manjeera had had a caesarean operation.

Two years went by quickly.

Nagesh asked the doctor, 'Please tell us if there is any special food or treatment for us to have a male child. This time we want only a male child.' The doctor got furious. 'No such methods. In any case, it is the xx chromosomes that are responsible for having a girl child. The woman is not responsible. You have to accept whoever is born this time,' she counselled him.

Manjeera was on hormonal treatment this time as well. The medicines caused vomiting, nausea and giddiness. When she complained with tearful eyes, the doctor looked at her helplessly and said, 'Go for the family planning operation this time, whether you give birth to a boy or a girl, Manjeera.' Nagesh almost scolded her, 'Nothing will happen. Can't you bear this much for a son?' Manjeera conceived again. Nagesh was elated.

The medical check-up revealed that Manjeera had high blood pressure. The doctor told her, 'Take the medicines regularly for hypertension. Come to me immediately if you have swelling in the feet or giddiness or seizures.'

Manjeera's blood pressure shot up to 200 in the third month of pregnancy and she had a miscarriage. She became weak due to heavy loss of blood. Nagesh was disappointed. The doctor told him that Manjeera had to be careful for one year and she should not conceive immediately. But Nagesh did not take the advice. Manjeera conceived within six months. This time too she had high blood pressure. She was taking medicines. Her entire body was swollen like a balloon. Nagesh kept warning her, 'Be careful, protect your pregnancy at least this time and give birth to an heir for me.'

There was no maid at home. Manjeera had to do all the work from sweeping the courtyard to doing the dishes. If ever Shyamala told Nagesh that Manjeera was unable to manage the housework and he should get a maid, he dismissed her, saying, 'Why Attayya? What work is there? How will she get exercise if she doesn't do that much work? She will do it slowly.' It was only when Shyamala went there sometimes that Manjeera got any rest. This pregnancy proved deadly for Manjeera. The foetus' movements stopped in the fifth month, but Manjeera did not know that. She went to the doctor in the sixth month. Her blood pressure had shot up to 230. The scan revealed that the foetus had died twenty days ago. It had degenerated inside.

The pregnancy was immediately aborted and her uterus cleaned. It was a close encounter with death for Manjeera. The doctor firmly told Nagesh, 'One more pregnancy will be fatal for her. She won't survive. So, she should not conceive. Either you take her for the family planning operation, or you get a vasectomy done.' She flared up, saying, 'You have a daughter. You can bring her up well. Is it mandatory for

Manjeera to give birth to your heir? Is her body a machine or is she a guinea pig in the lab?'

Manjeera's body felt like a wound, with a caesarean delivery, high blood pressure and two abortions in the span of five years. She felt intimidated at the very word pregnancy. She cried when she had the second abortion, saying that she wouldn't be able to take it any more. All the family members met for a discussion and decided to firmly tell Nagesh that he should immediately stop pressurizing Manjeera for a male heir.

'They won't listen if you tell them, Amma. It's their wish. Don't say anything,' said Manjeera, scared.

'It would be deadly for you if we keep quiet, Manji,' said Shyamala.

'Whatever it is, don't say anything. It's their wish,' Manjeera wept.

Shyamala fumed, 'Let's go. I will get the tubectomy done for you. We won't tell them.' She said this though she knew that the husband's signature and permission were mandatory.

'No Amma, they won't allow it,' said Manjeera, still scared.

SHYAMALA WENT BACK home after Manjeera recovered a bit. After that, Manjeera did not go to her parents' place, despite their repeated requests. Nor was there any information from her. Even when Shyamala called her, either her phone would be switched off or there would be no response. Her son-in-law said either that Manjeera was in the bathroom, had gone out or her phone was not working. When Shyamala's sons sent her WhatsApp messages, Manjeera was cryptic saying I am all right, yes, no, okay. Sometimes Nagesh let her talk to them on his phone when he was around. She would briefly say yes or no. It looked like she was hiding something from them. Shyamala asked, 'Why such monosyllabic answers even to your brothers on WhatsApp, Manjeera?' She said, detached, 'I am not sending those messages, my husband does. The phone is not in my hands at all.'

When Shyamala asked her to come along with her daughter, Manjeera said, 'Not possible, a lot of work for me. My mother-in-law is not well.' Gradually she put a full stop to even those brief conversations. Nagesh simply replied she was well or not well to their queries. Manjeera came home after almost a year on her grandmother's death. She was looking heavy. But she was chubby and wore salwar-kameez. So Shyamala could not make out anything. Her cousin, Kamala, said, 'She is hiding something. Please find out.'

Manjeera did not reply to Shyamala's persistent questions. Nagesh would be on guard all the time. He never allowed her to meet her mother alone. Manjeera was trying to escape from them, frightened. She slept all through the three days she was there.

Shyamala could not control herself anymore and asked Nagesh, 'Is she pregnant?' He said that she had put on weight due to her overeating.

One day, Manjeera quickly swallowed a tablet which she took out of her purse, thinking that no one was watching her.

When Shyamala asked her about the tablet, Nagesh came

running anxiously and said, 'Nothing Attayya – she takes a birth control pill every day.'

Shyamala angrily said, 'What is this Nagesh? Doesn't Manjeera feel giddy when she takes those medicines? How many years will you make her take those tablets? As the doctor said, either you get her operated or you get it done.'

Nagesh looked away, saying, 'Okay Attayya,' and left with his wife and daughter. He said, 'I have an urgent meeting in the office.' Manjeera followed her husband like a dumb cow, turning back and looking at her mother.

By the time Shyamala could leave the memories of her daughter behind, it was morning. The cock was crowing.

Two months passed.

One day, Shyamala was sitting near the entrance and winnowing millets. Her eldest son, Hithesh, was at home as it was a holiday. Hithesh was a well-known veterinary surgeon in the village. The neighbour Narsaiah came running, alarmed. 'Doctor saab, please come fast. Our Lakshmi is in labour since last night.' Hithesh took his gloves and started. Shyamala too curiously went to see them.

Lakshmi was Narsaiah's buffalo's name. She was in labour, moaning with pain. Hithesh examined her and said, 'The feet are down. It's been a long labour. I can save only one life. Tell me if you want the mother or the child.'

Narsaiah said in a choking voice, 'Look Doc saab, I have looked after her as my daughter, though she's a buffalo. The mother's life is more important for me. Let her live. Doesn't matter if the child does not survive.'

Hithesh said, 'Okay then, take her to the hospital fast. I will also come.' Narsaiah immediately took Lakshmi to the hospital. Hithesh reached the hospital in fifteen minutes.

SHYAMALA ASKED HITHESH when he reached home, 'What happened dear, did you kill the calf?'

'Yes Amma, had to kill the calf to save the mother,' said Hithesh. Shyamala said, 'Such a pity.'

Her phone rang, showing Manjeera's name. Shyamala happily took the call. 'Manji, are you all right dear?'

Manjeera said feebly, 'Amma, I am not able to manage. Please come Amma.'

Shyamala asked, dreading, 'What happened Manjeera?'

There was silence on the other side.

Shyamala apprehensively asked her again, 'Manjeera, tell me child, what happened?'

Manjeera said, 'I am pregnant Amma, ninth month.'

Shyamala could not comprehend for a minute, 'What are you talking about, Manjeera?'

'They did not listen to me, Amma. They want a son. I was in the sixth month when I came on grandmother's death,' Manjeera was sobbing.

'Ayyo, didn't the doctor tell you not to conceive again?' said Shyamala.

'Do these people listen to me, Amma? For them, their male heir is more important than my life,' Manjeera was crying in a feeble voice. 'They threatened that I should not reveal anything. They didn't allow me to talk on the phone or go out,' Manjeera continued.

'DIDN'T THE DOCTOR warn you against it, Nagesh? What is this again? Vadina (sister-in-law), don't you at least have any concern?' Shyamala angrily questioned Nagesh and his mother.

Nagesh's mother said, 'We warned her, Vadina. It's your daughter who wanted a male heir. We told her to adopt our youngest grandson. What can we do?'

Nagesh said with head bent, 'Yes Attayya, we continued only after the Hyderguda Charles hospital people said that they would rescue the mother and the child even if it is the tenth delivery in such cases.'

'Isn't our old doctor, Rekha, around?' asked Shyamala.

Nagesh replied that she had gone to America.

That night Manjeera whispered into her mother's ear, 'Amma, I didn't want the pregnancy. I said no. They didn't listen to me even when I pleaded with them that I wouldn't be able to.' Shyamala felt as if on that dark night, the moonlight came through the window and revealed some blurred secret hidden in Manjeera's eyes. Shyamala's heart missed a beat. As in the past, Manjeera had high blood pressure this time too. She was gasping for breath, unable to sit or stand. Shyamala couldn't control her grief when Manjeera said now and then, 'Amma, I am scared. Don't know if I will survive this time or not.'

Hithesh shouted at Nagesh on the phone, 'Do you have

any sense, Bava (brother-in-law)? Why did you do this, despite knowing that pregnancy was dangerous for her life?' Nagesh said, 'Bava, she is fine,' as if he was not concerned.

'The total package is for four lakh rupees. The baby is underweight, at 700 grams. Very little amniotic fluid. The mother has high blood pressure. She certainly has to be in the hospital for one month. If necessary, the Charles hospital would terminate the pregnancy and rescue the mother,' the doctor counselled them. The doctor said, 'Very bad obstetric history. She is at high risk,' and asked Nagesh to sign on the consent sheet.

Nagesh said, 'We'll think about it and get back to you,' and came out with his wife. 'They will kill the child, it seems. But they want four lakh rupees.' Nagesh started the moped impatiently and hollered at Manjeera, 'Sit now.'

Manjeera got on and sat on the vehicle like a dumb entity.

Shyamala said, 'I'll give the money, Nagesh. Somehow we will raise the remaining money.' Nagesh angrily said, 'What is the use Attayya – they will kill the child if necessary.'

Shyamala said, 'They're big doctors. They know what to do and what not to do. Let them do their job.'

Nagesh kept quiet.

Manjeera silently curled up in bed. She felt as if the male child rooted in her womb was sucking all her blood and making her helpless.

'Very bad obstetric history, Amma. The record of Manjeera's previous pregnancies is not good at all. I don't understand how she could carry the pregnancies with such high blood pressure. Manjeera is in a dangerous condition. I'm admitting her because you have come with trust in me. I am also worried,' said Dr Sulochana. Shyamala's heart missed a beat on hearing a doctor with forty years' experience say that. Shyamala held her, crying, 'Somehow save the mother and the child, doctor.'

Manjeera was given glucose until the amniotic fluid in her womb increased. The foetus also grew a little. Based on the scan, the doctor said Manjeera had to go for an emergency caesarean operation.

THE BABY BOY weighing 800 gram was sent to the paediatric hospital.

Nagesh's and his people's happiness knew no bounds. 'Thank god, the heir has been born,' said Nagesh's aunt.

Nagesh's uncle said, 'You protected our honour by giving birth to a son.'

Manjeera was sitting on the bed like a white pigeon. Her face looked calm and fresh. 'Amma, a baby girl would have been better. They would have learned a lesson,' she said.

Shyamala heaved a sigh, 'He was born, and he saved you. Or else they would have asked you to conceive again and again.'

Manjeera was discharged after a week. Her blood pressure came down to normal. Everyone, including the doctor, felt relieved. Even so, the doctor warned her repeatedly, 'You should be careful,' and discharged her.

In that blazing sun in the scorching summer heat,

Manjeera would go to the children's hospital on a moped, feed the child and also give him warmth by keeping him close to her bosom.

Shyamala grieved looking at her daughter, who had just delivered a child and yet had to climb twenty steps every day. When she said, 'Take her in a cab, Nagesh,' he replied, 'I've booked one, Attayya.' But he took her on his moped to save on the cab fare.

FOR FIFTEEN DAYS after the delivery, Manjeera went to the hospital every day, fed the son, took him into her lap for some time and came back. She was afraid of her boy who resembled a tiny baby monkey.

One morning, Manjeera was getting ready to visit her son and went for a bath. But she quickly wore a nightie and came out, complaining of giddiness.

She complained of pain in the middle of the back. Shyamala got her to sit on the cot, rubbed her back and enquired if she had taken the tablet for high blood pressure. Manjeera said yes. Shyamala requested Nagesh to call the ambulance. Manjeera had already been suffering for twenty minutes. Shyamala knew that the miserly Nagesh was delaying. She called to book the ambulance herself. Shyamala could tell that Manjeera had chest pain.

Manjeera suddenly got up, collapsed, wriggled and her eyes turned up. Shyamala shook up Manjeera, feeling for her breath under her nose and calling out to her frantically. But Manjeera was gone by then. Nagesh took Manjeera's head into his lap and shook her, saying, 'Manji, give me some time. I'll take you to a good doctor.' But Manjeera's sojourn on this earth was over by then. Manjeera gave Nagesh an heir, and left him her body wounded with septic abortions, caesareans and high blood pressure. She left the right to cremate her dead body to Nagesh. Shyamala collapsed in grief and fury.

SHYAMALA SCREAMED, 'No, no post-mortem please, don't cut my daughter.' It was already an hour since Manjeera had passed away. The doctor said that the reason for her death was unknown and as it was a suspicious death, a post-mortem had to be done. Shyamala wailed, 'No, she died in front of our eyes. Don't cut my daughter. She went through hell as long as she was alive. Let her be peaceful at least after death.' Nagesh lit Manjeera's pyre. His face had gone pale.

Shyamala was beating her chest, looking at her daughter's pyre with unbearable grief. She cursed Nagesh, 'You're the one who killed my daughter, you demon!'

'AMMA,' HITHESH GRIEVED. He was reminded of people like Narsaiah, who saved Lakshmi's life, prioritizing the mother's life. He was shaken with sorrow, 'You should have got the post-mortem done, Amma. We would have known the reason for Chelli's (younger sister) death. That fellow murdered my Chelli, Amma; I won't let go of him. I will consult a lawyer.'

A new mother was raising Nagesh's motherless son on her breast milk, in the hospital.

§

ten

My Husband Raped Me

I WORK AS A MEDICAL OFFICER at the Vignan Jyothi hospital. The other day, I was late for duty and the patients were waiting. One of them, Ramadevi, stood up eagerly when she saw me. She had reports in her hand and some fear in her eyes. I don't know how long she had been waiting. Hers was the first appointment.

Ramadevi's eyes were filled with fear and sorrow when she asked me, 'Madam, are the reports normal? Is there any problem?' What could I tell her? The report was positive for a venereal disease called herpes. Her wayward husband had passed his disease onto her.

Ramadevi had come to the hospital three days before that. She had said that she had been getting pearl-like boils around her genitals for the past one year. She had pain and itching. Whenever she got such boils, her husband said it was due to excess of heat and brought some creams. Her husband also used to get such boils. Three days ago, she had come to the hospital without his knowledge. I understood the problem as soon as I examined her. I got the viral screening test done and told her about the report. Ramadevi's face turned red. 'Bastard, every time he swears by the children. A few days ago, my brother-in-law saw him in a hotel with a girl and told me. I made up my mind and came to you. What should I do now, Madam?' Ramadevi's voice was trembling with grief.

'You should use medicines. This is a very stubborn disease. Even if it comes down, it will keep recurring. First, stop him from doing such things. Discuss this with your parents and parents-in-law. If he continues like this, he might even pass on AIDS to you.' I told her that they should use condoms every time. She went away with head bent, tears welling up in her eyes. I gave her the address of a women's organization. I see almost ten women like Ramadevi in a week. Every time, it only makes me angry.

Next, somebody was hurriedly brought in on a stretcher. I rushed towards her. A girl who was sixteen or seventeen years old. She was looking scared to death and was trembling all over. She was sobbing and calling out 'Amma, Amma.' There was mehendi on her hands and a glittering new nuptial thread around her neck. She was wearing green and red bangles, together with one golden bangle, on each hand. The glass bangles were broken and her hands were bleeding. The traces of blood on her feet were mixed with mehendi and turmeric. Something that should not have happened had happened. Her hair was ruffled. Scratches, bruises, scars on her eyebrows, lips, ears, chin, cheeks – all over the face. Her lower lip was split and there was a blood clot on it. There were scratches on her hands and agony in her eyes, and tears were welling up in her fearful eyes. She was accompanied probably by her in-laws. I asked them what had happened to her. 'Nothing, a small tiff between the couple,' the man replied nonchalantly, looking at me as if asking, 'How are you concerned?'

'What is she to you?' I asked.

'My daughter-in-law – son's wife. Ten days since they have been married,' he was irritated. The mother-in-law said, 'See her quickly, madam. It won't look nice if her parents come.' I could make out that they wouldn't give any details and decided to ask her, instead. I instructed the staff to take her to the casualty ward and I followed.

I examined her first. There was severe bleeding from the genitals and a three-inch tear. She was trembling all over. Her thighs, knees and legs were shaking. She was almost in shock. I could make out her condition. I made her lie down on the operation table and asked her cajolingly, 'What happened? Tell me, dear.' She shivered with grief. She controlled herself and said, 'My husband raped me and bashed me.' I was surprised. 'Rape? Your husband?' I asked her. She nodded her head to say yes.

I STARTED TO PERFORM the operation first. The bleeding had to stop, or else she would slip into shock. I didn't know how much blood she had lost at home. I quickly sutured the torn vagina. Medicines were being given to her with intravenous fluids. Her waist trembled when I sutured the wound. That beast had wounded her so badly that her vagina was split into two. My heart was drenched in grief. A young girl, still a child, a minor by age…how could that beast do this? Did the beast have a heart?

I sent her to the radiology department. Her hand was fractured. Then I got her shifted to a room.

'MADAM, MY NAME IS Satvika. I was married fifteen days ago. I wanted to study. But they did not allow me to continue my Intermediate and got me married. I am scared of him. He is fifteen years older than me. I shivered at the very thought of the nuptial night. Fortunately, I got my periods. I escaped for five days. On the sixth day, they arranged the nuptial night. I fainted as soon as he touched me. I escaped for two more days. I was frightened. I slept in my mother-in-law's room. My father-in-law called my father and scolded him, saying, "You didn't teach your daughter anything. She trembles at the sight of her husband. My son's life seems to have been destroyed." The next time, too, I fainted but my husband bashed me up when I came to consciousness, holding me by the hair and kicking me in my ribs. I fainted again.

'I lost hope and ran away to my parents' place without letting them know. My father beat me up and bashed up my mother too, blaming her for not bringing me up well. He threw me at my father-in-law's feet and said, "This is your girl; you can do whatever you want to," and left.

145

'That day also they sent me into the room. Before that, my mother-in-law warned me, saying, "It won't be all right if you repeat what you were doing." My sister-in-law scolded me, saying, "Don't destroy my younger brother's life. Am I not leading a life with my husband? I am only four years older than you."

'When my husband tried to hug me, I got scared and said I had my periods and my stomach was aching. He said, "No problem, nothing will happen to men even if women have their periods when they get together," and pulled me towards him. I was scared about what would happen if he came to know that I was lying. I had thought that he would let me go if I said I had my period. I moved away from him and requested him to leave me alone as it wouldn't be possible as far as I was concerned. That was it – he got furious. He started beating me crazily. He beat me with his hands, legs, a stick and a belt. He kept beating me for half an hour. I kept crying, fell at his feet and begged him to stop beating me. But he did not. When he pushed me angrily, I fell on the window and broke my hand. Meanwhile, my mother-in-law and sister-in-law had also come in. My father-in-law came in and scolded me, saying, "Kill the bitch." My mother-in-law sent him out and told her son to lay me down on the cot. She slapped me, saying, "You bitch, how long will you harass my son? He is a good man so he kept you here and tolerated you." My husband lifted me and threw me onto the cot. My sister-in-law held my hands tight and my mother-in-law my legs. "Go on, let's see how she will escape today. Get the work done, son," she said. My husband stuffed a cloth in my mouth and fell on me like a beast. Blood was streaming down. I curled up with pain. The bed sheet was drenched in blood. They thought I might die, so they changed my clothes and brought me to the hospital. Madam, my father handed me over to them. I won't live with them, madam.' Satvika tried to lift her hands, but screamed in pain.

I looked at her X-ray reports. Her wrist bone was fractured. I sent word to the orthopaedic doctor. My heart was burning with grief and anger at her story. Meanwhile, Satvika's parents came. Her mother held Satvika and howled. She looked at her husband and screamed, 'You didn't listen to me when I said don't send the girl to that beast. Are you a human being at all?' I pacified her and told her to file an FIR in the police station.

Satvika's father said angrily, 'What are you talking about, Doctoramma? Had this girl obliged her husband, would it have gone this far? Why else does one have a wife? Can you call a woman a woman if she cannot give pleasure to her husband?'

I was surprised. I looked at Satvika's mother. I thought of the amount of violence she must have endured with this man. At that moment, she looked like a furnace hiding the hot coals. 'Stop it. You are still blaming the child instead of questioning them for assaulting her. What I have experienced with you is enough. My child will not take it, what do you think! I will complain to the police. How much blood she has lost! Bastards, how can they beat her to the extent of breaking her bones?' the mother yelled at her husband, threatening him with her index finger, her eyes red. The fire was escaping from the furnace.

I angrily told her father-in-law, 'The husband has no right to have sex without the wife's consent. He has not only raped her, but bashed her till her bones are broken. Wounds and scratches all over her body. Her vagina is deeply cut. She has lost a lot of blood.' Her in-laws were looking daggers at me. The father-in-law angrily said, 'The husband slept with his wife and you are calling it rape. What is this Doctoramma – have you gone mad? Let's go Venkatreddy, get her discharged. Let's take her home.'

He pulled his wife along with him, warning Satvika's father that she should be home by that evening. 'You are calling it rape Doctoramma. Has my son-in-law raped some other woman? No, he slept with his wife. Satvika is his wife. He can do whatever he wants to do,' said her father. As I was explaining to them that rape is a crime even if it is with one's wife, the local sub-inspector entered. I had called her secretly.

Satvika's father was taken aback and screamed, 'This is a domestic matter. Why did the police come here? Go away. I won't make any complaint.' The sub-inspector sent him out first. Meanwhile, I saw Satvika's in-laws going out of the hospital.

The sub-inspector closed the doors, checked the medical reports and surgical reports and noted everything, including my version. She went up to Satvika and asked, 'What happened, tell me?' Satvika said boldly and clearly,

'My husband raped me.' I stepped out of the room. Women, pregnant women, were waiting for me with reports in their hands and grief in their eyes.

§

eleven

The Fall of Man

'**M**Y STUDENTS ARE ENACTING the play "Adam and Eve: The Fall of Man" on this Women's Day, with some changes. Our male colleagues will, as usual, cry to death,' Meenakshi said with a naughty smile.

Mandakini chuckled and said, 'Such adventures are usual for you, aren't they?'

Both of them were in their fifties. Mandakini was a Professor of Telugu, while Meenakshi was a Professor of Gender Studies. They had been working in the same university campus for the past twenty years. They were bound together by a thick friendship, sans pretentions. It was routine for them to meet every day in the canteen over coffee.

'YOU WRETCHED MAN, Adam! I placed you in this heaven-like Eden Garden and created the woman for you from your ribs. You did not follow my condition that you can eat all

150

fruits in this garden and drink sweet water, but cannot eat the fruit of this knowledge tree. I will curse you now,' God was furious.

Scared, Adam hid behind the tree. He wasn't coming out. He had tied fig leaves around his waist. He was ashamed of his nakedness. He was not like that before. Why was Adam feeling ashamed now? God had left him completely naked. God's anger was mounting every minute.

'You are the one who created me. Did I ask you to create this woman for me? Look, she passed on the knowledge fruit to me. She gave me only a small piece and ate the rest of it. Soon after that, I felt ashamed and scared, and a sense that this nakedness was not all right. She covered herself with leaves and covered me with the same.' Adam pointed towards the woman, trembling.

'What is my mistake, Lord? That serpent told me to eat that fruit. It said that if I eat that fruit, I will also learn to distinguish between good, bad, shame and fear, like you can. It asked, "How long will you continue to be shameless like this? That Lord is conspiring against you so that you don't become wise." I, too, felt that it was right. In any case, how can you create me from the man's rib and create the man specially from mud? Don't I have a separate identity and existence?' Eve was angry, her eyes turned red.

'No, in fact, you are a bone of the man's bone and flesh of his flesh. You don't have a separate existence. You have to be in the man, with the man and for the man. Despite creating you from the man's bone, you caused this calamity. What would have happened if I created you specially?' the Lord screamed in anger.

'This is even better. You are shouting that you created me from the man's bone. But the scientist, Jewett, says that I was created from the man's genital. Without us women and our uterus, even you cannot take birth. Men's identity is in women. See, you taught Adam to live without shame. I covered him with these leaves and taught him shame. What is wrong?' Provoked, Eve yelled. 'But this serpent did a good thing,' Eve pointed towards the serpent that was waving its hood, and smiled. She jumped up to pluck one more fig leaf and tied it around Adam's waist.

God looked daggers at the serpent and raised his eyebrows, as if questioning it.

'Can you leave humans in this blind universe without shame and distinction between good and bad? Especially women? Can you create Eve as Adam's companion, to cook for him, to give birth to children and to entertain him? As for the condition that the fruit of knowledge should not be tasted, it would benefit you if all your people were fools, wouldn't it?' the serpent said, heaving.

God was mad with anger. He kicked Adam, saying, 'You paid no heed to my words, fell into this woman's spell and degraded yourself, though you are a man. I kick you down to the mud-filled earth from this heavenly garden of Eden. Go!' Adam tumbled down to the earth.

'Now you Eve, you caused the fall of the man whom I created. You will run this creation by harvesting crops, cooking in the man's house, slogging and suffering deadly labour pangs throughout your life. Not only that, I am giving the man authority and power over you,' God brayed.

'Now you, you will be lying limbless in the mud and eating mud. I make you the enemy of the whole of mankind. You will be harming each other,' he said, looking at the serpent.

The serpent and Eve howled with laughter. God was taken aback.

'Was your magic successful in heaven for it to succeed on earth? We will be much more conscious on earth. You are not the one who will write my fate, but it is the writer of this play who has rewritten our story. Anyway, Adam, the man you created, fell not because of me, but because of you. He came onto the right path because of me. We will teach him, the man you created, how to conduct himself with respect for women, dignity, and shame on the earth too.' Eve and the serpent jumped onto the earth holding hands.

God was shocked. With regret, he thought, 'I should have first prevented the serpent from entering this garden and then created the shameless naked Adam.' He left crying, with sorrow on his face.

The curtains came down. The hall echoed with applause. Darshitha, who played Eve, rushed towards Meenakshi, calling out to her, 'Madam'. Meenakshi complimented her, 'Well done! You really did well.' Darshitha's face gleamed with joy and self-confidence.

DARSHITHA WAS IN LOVE with a boy. They had known each

other for three years. Her parents objected to their alliance, saying that the boy was a North Indian and was not suitable for her. They got her married to an engineer in their own community. Darshitha gave up her love for her parents. But the husband almost raped her on their nuptial night. She suffered severe bleeding. The husband was like a beast. She could not bear the wounds that he caused by raping her under the licence of the sacred thread. She decided that he was not fit to be her companion, separated from him and continued her education, which had been discontinued. The marriage counsellor motivated her to join the gender studies course to understand the source of her husband's authority that gave him licence to assault her.

'I really admire Darshitha. She left the husband who sexually assaulted her once. She called him unfit for marital life. But what about us? Are we not continuing to bear it?' said Meenakshi, looking intently at Mandakini's face. Mandakini sighed and said, leaving, 'I have an appointment with the gynaecologist. I have to go. Bye.'

HE WAS OUT OF STATION. He would not come back till the next two or three days. She too was on vacation. She was enjoying her privacy in his absence. But her heart, which was wounded by him, was fluttering like a string stuck in a desert shrub, unable to disentangle itself.

'Amma, how are you? How is Nanna? Are you fighting with each other like always? My salary has been hiked, Amma. I have applied for H1 again. Yes, yes. Trump has come to power now; I don't know what he will do. What is to be done – I will come back to India. No worries. I too joined the women's wing here the other day. I participated in the dharna against Trump's obscene blabbering against women. Okay Amma, go to the doctor regularly.'

Tapasya's voice was like the uninterrupted flow of a river. Had she not been putting up with his offensive behaviour only for Tapasya! Till recently, till five years ago, he was all right. His attitude towards her changed after her menopause. He looked at her as if she was a useless pot with a hole.

Fed up, Mandakini walked into the balcony with some unknown anxiety, to escape from something. There were fields beside the house. There was a forest with thick trees beside the fields. They had constructed that house thinking that it would be peaceful on the outskirts of the city. But where was the peace? How long should she have to endure a marital life without love, affection and kindness?

Mandakini sat in an easy chair. She bound herself to darkness and solitude. It looked as if the sky had bent to look probingly at Mandakini's face with its eyes of stars. She hugged a small pillow to her bosom and slowly closed her eyes. With her eyelids closed, darkness poured into her. She was reminded of Eve fighting with the Lord in the play 'The Fall of Man'.

'Why did you create me only for the man, only for Adam? Why didn't you create me as an independent being? That's why I ate this fruit of knowledge and became wise,' Eve had guffawed.

Mandakini woke up to that laughter.

How nice it would be if he hugged her to his chest and said that he continued to love her! Not just him, many people did not know that the bodies of women who have stopped menstruating or have lost the uterus should be understood in harmony with their hearts. This man did not know at all. Did her identity mean only her body, only the vagina and the depths of the uterus of changing hormones, dried up like her heart!

He tried to tell her what she was and defined her in a certain manner, and gave her nonsensical advice as to what to do and what not to do. She felt like saying, 'Only I know about my condition. Why do I need your advice? I will speak about my condition. I know that this condition is caused by the changes in the hormones in my body.' But would he understand that? Why couldn't he, on his own, share her anger, impulsiveness, sorrow, depression and irritation? Why couldn't he draw her close to him and cajole her? Even if he was not always with her, why couldn't he assure her that he was with her during her crisis?

Instead, why did he yell at her, telling her that she should change? Till recently, she was what she was. She definitely changed due to the change in hormones. But did he change because of his hormones or because of his male attitude? Was he playing with her like this because of his suddenly aggravated sex hormones? He always told her to understand him. He could have taken her out for dinner. He could have gifted her brushes and colours to continue her old hobby of painting. He could have been with her to pave the path for her journey towards menopause, leading her towards a new psychological and physical condition. Wouldn't she have appreciated him a great deal then?

Suddenly Mandakini was reminded of Professor Lakshmi's words.

'If the wife reaches menopause, it is mid-life crisis for the husband. Many husbands turn into traitors against their wives. Be careful. Anyway, it is not as though our husbands are under our control.' Professor Lakshmi had heaved a sigh. Mandakini did not know what suffering she was going through because of her husband!

By any chance, was her husband also betraying her? She didn't know. The twenty-five-year-old widow, Savithri, sometimes came home with the office files. How greedily he stared at her body from head to toe. He said proudly, raising his eyebrows, 'Do you know her age? Twenty-five years.' As if Savithri's age stopped there and only her's increased. Had she asked about Savithri's age? What did he look for in Savithri's body? The youth that she had lost? Hadn't he lost his youth too? Did he ever look into her eyes? Did he look at her at all? Was he aware that he was also in menopause, like her?

Mandakini was reminded of Dr Jyothi's words.

When she had asked her if men did not have menopause, Dr Jyothi had laughed loudly and said, 'Why not? Their disease is called ADAM, that is, androgen deficiency of the ageing male. It is also called andropause. The male sex hormones start decreasing in these people. They think we don't know about it. Their desires also come down in middle age. Less energy, depression, anger, impulses, mood swings, weakening muscles, fat accumulation at the waist, hips, tummy, face and neck, hot flushes, like we go through. The erections are also not complete.'

'My husband behaves as if everything is fine with him. Takes vitamins at night. Where is his youth, doctor? He shamelessly says and shows, "Look how much power I have and how firm it is,"' she said angrily.

'They may not be vitamins. Next time when you come, bring the prescription and the medicines that he uses. I'll tell you,' said Dr Jyothi. Mandakini tried to reduce the pain she felt at how her husband looked down on her by sharing it with the doctor.

She emerged from these memories.

She was reminded of her colleague Meenakshi and the way she had been treated disparagingly. She was reminded of how ardently she shared her knowledge of gender studies with her students. Meenakshi's husband, Shekhar, had left her to live with a woman who was half his age. He might very soon send her the divorce notice. Five years ago, when fibroids were detected in Meenakshi's uterus, it was removed to prevent any danger. Along with the uterus, the ovaries that release female hormones were also removed. He always ridiculed her with, 'You're an empty pot. You have no femininity. You don't look like a woman to me at all. Everything of yours is dried up.' Meenakshi said, 'I told him that I'll divorce him after my daughter's marriage. I can't tolerate him.' Meenakshi's skin looked dry due to the hormone deficiency. Her eyes had an empty, parched look. These men want their wives to always have a soft, bright youthfulness and firm bodies. How can human bodies not wither and bend? Are the men not ageing? Do they continue to have a soft, strong, wide chest, dark hair on their chest reflecting their *mardanagi* (maleness – this is the word he uses), a flat stomach and unbent shoulders? He looked ugly as if a pot has been turned upside down; he looked nine months pregnant.

When he fell on her like a bear with that stomach, she felt suffocated under the weight of that layered fat. Even if she delicately pushed him away with a thumping heart, he would become hysterical with anger and turn away, sulking and taking it as a rejection.

It was not as if she was ageing and he was frozen in youth. His sex hormones had decreased, some hormones had either stopped functioning or worn out or withdrawn or swollen; gray hair mixed with black hair – on hands, eyebrows, nose, ears, beard, chest – all over the body, he looked like a bear. Did she ever say, 'You look ugly and I don't feel any desire for you?' Anyway, when did she feel any desire for him? Oh, what hell it was for her to see him naked like a beast! How many times had he told her that he could not bear to see her like a swollen bottle gourd with truck-like tyres hanging around the waist! Didn't he have the same tyres of fat?

He talked to her like Meenakshi's husband did to her. But, she never replied to him the way Meenakshi replied to her husband.

Mandakini's eyelids fell, tired and weak.

Would he ever understand? She herself was unable to understand her body after she stopped menstruating. How would he understand? She could clearly understand the changes in his body and mind. He kept talking about the body all the time. He used words like withering, fading and drying, and mourned over how his sex life had ended at the age of fifty-four, saying, 'Oh, you have dried up totally.' Did all men react like this? Or did he have some genetic problem?

Suddenly she remembered her mother-in-law, Suguna. She had to satisfy her husband's desire whether it was at a festival or during her periods, whether she was running a temperature or the grown-up children were watching, and even when she went to her parents' house or for some marriage. Otherwise, she was battered and abused. Obscene accusations like, 'You are refusing. Who are you seeing?' She couldn't escape. One day, she cried, 'Mandakini, I can't take it. Why is your father-in-law obsessed with it at this age? I don't have the energy. Get some medicine for him or else I will consume something and die.' Finally, her wish came true. Her husband died of prostate cancer. Suguna sat beside her husband's dead body but did not shed a single tear. She looked very peaceful. Whatever she felt, Mandakini thought her mother-in-law would be able to live peacefully from then on. Her husband was also obsessed, exactly like his father.

Unable to sleep, Mandakini rolled impatiently. She could not sleep at all at night. Early in her marriage, she could not sleep, with the children weeping, having to clean the mess made by them and having to cater to his desire. When the children started growing up, their college timings changed. Then they had night shifts. She had to shift her schedule to be there for them at night instead of the morning. She would wait till three in the morning to make sure they had some food. Due to all this, her sleep cycle was disturbed. Now that the children had grown up and flown away, she wanted to sleep. She had the time to sleep. But the hormones were dancing in her brain. Added to that, the wounds of humiliation that her husband subjected her to came back to her at night and ruined her sparse sleep. Sleep, sleep, slumber, where are you? Where had she slipped away from her mother's lap? How she wished somebody would put her to sleep! Her brain rested only if she took a Restyl tablet, prescribed by her doctor. Or else her eyes ached with the weight of her eyelids, which were wide open all through the night. The doctor told her not to think. She took Calmpose, Zolfresh or Restyl a hundred times to pacify the scorpions and centipedes crawling on her eyelids of disturbed sleep. These have become the therapy for women's sleeplessness.

The puzzled doctor said, 'What do you think about?' and added unasked, 'The children have grown up; you should relax now.' Instead of going into the root of the problem, these doctors dismissed the problem by saying that women's stupidity is the cause of their psychological, physical and sexual problems and sleeplessness.

Even if they knew, they were not bothered because they were men. How could she not think? He called her dried up. Complained of burning when he entered her. He did not think how painful it was for her. He complained of not feeling the fullness of her breasts since they were sagging. He said that his desire died when he saw her and that the white-skinned neighbour, Suneetha, intoxicated him more than her. He even entered her house on the pretext of meeting her father-in-law, Janaki Ramaiah, and returned sighing. He blabbered that twenty-five-year-old Nalini, who was almost his daughter's age, drove him crazy in office.

He said that she had reached her menopause but, in fact, she suspected that he was impotent. Sometimes he was weary and turned away, exhausted. But he became a typhoon when he used the vitamins and her condition became miserable. She couldn't understand this. What were those vitamins and were those vitamins in the first place? Dr Jyothi had said no. Mandakini slowly got up and searched for his prescription. She found the prescription and the tablets. The tablets said 'Suhagra'.

Was that the same as the Viagra that she had heard of? Mandakini decided to ask Dr Jyothi.

'THESE ARE NOT vitamin tablets at all, madam! These are Viagra tablets. Men who have reached andropause use these to prolong erection. Definitely, your husband is using these and having sex with you. He is concealing his lack,' said Dr Jyothi.

Mandakini was furious.

She felt humiliated. She was reminded of her entire past,

afresh. When she stopped menstruating, the moisture in the layers of her heart and body evaporated. She remained like a dried up well or a river. Moreover, he secretly swallowed those horrible Viagra tablets and sharply cut her dried up body like a knife or a crowbar. How much burning it caused!

Her vagina was torn in the attacks that lasted about half an hour despite her objections, the passage of her dried up body became wet with blood, she bore the pain, pressing her lips under her teeth, shedding tears and writhing in pain. Her thighs and back ached unbearably. But he wouldn't stop. It was like pricking a needle into a wound. Who? Who? Which fellow in which company had discovered this to transform a man into a knife or a crowbar in order to dig a woman's delicate body to draw out streams of blood? Would he ever admit to using those tablets? When she asked him, he said they were vitamin tablets to overcome his weakness. He hid the prescription from her but somehow she had caught hold of it.

'What do I lack? It's you who have become useless, like a dried up well. You have reached menopause, but you weep like a virgin on the nuptial night. Do you think I can't find anyone else if you refuse? They will flock to me at the snap of a finger, do you know?' He talked threateningly to her when she clearly refused him sometimes, unable to bear the pain.

What arrogance in his eyes! The fellow in the company who discovered Viagra for these men should be torched. Did that fellow too take these tablets and torture his wife?

How atrocious it was! The sixty-eight-year-old

Dhanunjayarao, who lived on the third floor of an apartment building, lured the four-year-old daughter of Sagar and Menaka, who lived on the second floor and did small jobs, saying that he was like her grandfather, and sexually assaulted her. They caught him when he was running away after dropping the bleeding and unconscious child in front of her house. When the police arrested him and searched his house, they found porn CDs, porn sites on his computer, whisky bottles, condom packets and Viagra tablets. That child's body was torn into two in that beastly atrocity and she succumbed to the injuries. Her mother went out of her mind and had to be treated by a psychiatrist for several months. They had had this child six years after marriage. They sold their house and moved to some other district.

Mandakini firmly resolved, 'He went on a tour. Will return tonight. Today I should catch the thief. He has a lack in him. But he looks down upon me and humiliates me. I should turn this Viagra macho into a dead snake.'

'DADDY, WHY DON'T you understand my mother? She has reached menopause. Her irritation, anger, and peevishness are due to her hormonal imbalance. These are not mother's natural characteristics. The hormonal therapy will cure her. She needs your support as her partner at this stage, daddy! Be like a friend with mom!'

'Tell me the truth, dad! You have also grown old like my mother. Why do you behave as if only she has become old? Daddy, not just for mother, you too get your androgen profile done. See for yourself how imbalanced your sex hormones will be. No, you won't get it done. Mother's menstrual cycle has stopped. So, it's a proof. But, for you? Only mother will know for certain. She has really become frustrated with you. Instead of preventing her blood pressure from going up at this age, you are disturbing her all the more. She needs your help. I am speaking as a woman. I am worried, daddy, about what will happen to me if I am in that stage and if I get a husband like you! Please don't hurt mom, I beg you, dad! Take her for a walk. Get her soya food that increases her oestrogen hormone. Take her to movies and dinners. Assure her that you are with her.'

Mandakini could not control her tears. It was Tapasya's conversation with her father. He forgot to log out from his mail before he left.

IT WAS 9 O'CLOCK AT NIGHT. Mandakini was observing her husband smoking and loitering in the balcony. Her anger was increasing and her patience was waning. The Viagra prescription was getting squeezed in her fist. It mentioned ED (erectile dysfunction). He had ego problems apart from ED. That's why he got ED.

It was eleven at night.

Mandakini hugged him from behind. He moved uncomfortably. After a while, she started feeling him.

'What is this tummy like a pot turned upside down?' She stroked his stomach and hit him on the stomach. He was a little surprised and moved a little away from her. She moved closer. He tried to get up from the bed.

'Where are you going? Will you take Viagra and come? You are ever-young, aren't you? Why do you need Viagra?' She quickly got up, pulled his lungi and threw it into a corner of the room. He had become lean. He looked exactly like Adam, naked.

Mandakini roared till her eyes turned red and tears welled up.

Then she took out the Viagra tablets and the prescription that she had hidden in her blouse and flung them on his face. Somehow she felt like Eve, who had covered the man's nakedness and taught him shame. It's only that Eve covered Adam with a cloth and Mandakini took off the cloth of this Adam.

Mandakini's husband rushed to reach the lungi in the corner, quickly wrapped it around himself, and ran out of the room looking at his wife, who was roaring like a tigress in a rage.

twelve

§

The Kiss

COOL MOONLIGHT WAS SPREADING on the high mountains, making the green grass shine. The pearl-like white grass flowers were greeting the stars in the sky.

Those were the mountains where I played with my friends in my childhood and exulted looking at the white grass flowers. It was like that again now! He was pushing me against the mountain and bending over my face. The moonlight in his eyes was flowing towards me like the water gate-crashing the lake. His lips were as red as flowers of blood that were ready to split with desire. Who was he? I had seen him somewhere. I couldn't remember. He bent forward, took my face into his hands and softly caressed my forehead. He called me, 'Tapasvi', before he caressed me. How he took my face into his hands! It was like he was stretching his hands in devotion and receiving the food offered to god. He started to kiss my eyes, cheeks and chin silently and passionately. The touch of his lips was intoxicating. I couldn't resist him. He kept calling me as he kissed my lips. His heated lips were pouring honey into my being. My body started to pulsate. My mouth was filled with the sweetness of his kiss. He kept kissing me and whispering my name into my ear. The ocean of my body became one single wave and touched the skies.

Suddenly I woke up. Was it a dream? My body, drenched in sweat, was still responding. I looked around. Darkness, except the faint light of the bed lamp. My husband, Mahesh, was asleep. I don't know how late at night he had come home. I had waited till midnight and gone to sleep. He was smelling of alcohol. I was used to this. Slowly I got up from bed, walked into the veranda and sat on a chair. It was going to be three in the morning. The fragrance of the jasmine creeper outside the veranda grille was flowing in. That dream was magical. Mahesh turned our bed into a battlefield while making love. I never felt the ecstasy of that dream in all these years. How could I feel it with just one kiss? How strange! Who was he? I closed my eyes and slipped into deep thoughts. Those eyes...they were filled with cool moonlight; he had thick eyebrows, a sharp nose, curly hair and the open, smiling lips. Who? Dusky, shining complexion. Yes, it was him. The one who followed me like a shadow in my adolescence, expressed his love and got rejected by me. It was Sarangadhara, Saranga. I was thirteen years old then. He was probably sixteen. His father, Murthy uncle, lived behind my house. He was the oldest among the group of children who gathered in the colony park to play. He called me Tapsu, like the people in my house did. He laughed mischievously, saying, 'I call you Tappu because you always make mistakes. Your people also call you Tappu.' If I didn't go to play, he would send his sister, Swathi. She would drag me with her, saying that her brother had insisted that she bring me along. His face always lit up when he saw me. He would then ask me, 'What happened? Why didn't you come?' as if he were saying that you should certainly come for me. Once, all the children went to the hills in front of our house. The mountain that I saw in my dream was a memory of this. Exactly behind the hill, he caught hold of me and said, 'I love you Tapasvi,' and kissed my cheek. I quickly pushed him away and ran home with tears welling up in my eyes.

After that, I did not go there, even though he called me repeatedly, even though I liked him. Meanwhile, my father was transferred to Hyderabad and the family shifted there from Vijayawada and I completely forgot about him. I never thought of him in all these years. I saw him in this dream six years after my marriage…in this manner! Why? Why did my body respond so well, that too, to a kiss in the dream?

I closed my eyes and lay back, tired. Suddenly, a secret, sweet whisper in my ears called out 'Tapsu, Tapsu' and flowed into my heart. My heart missed a beat. I woke up from sleep. Yes, he called my name when he kissed me. How lovingly and longingly he touched me and kissed me! Was that the reason behind this beautiful sensation – calling out my name, my name alone and not anyone else's! I heard my husband, Mahesh, calling me. I felt exhausted at once. The sweetness

169

that the dream had left in its wake vanished. I felt devastated thinking about Mahesh. My heart was filled with revulsion. Tears welled up in my eyes. I had responded to the kiss of some other man in my dream and I experienced sensations that I have never felt in my husband's love. Why did this happen?

Like anyone else, I too had dreams about marriage, a loving husband, romance, children, a beautiful home. Mahesh fell in love with me and married me after convincing my parents. He was introduced to me at the wedding of my friend, Manasa, as her groom's friend. He was six feet tall, fair and handsome.

I noticed Mahesh staring at me during the wedding. He followed me like a shadow and greeted me with his eyes. I thought he was impressed with my beauty. Mahesh took that familiarity ahead and gave me a love letter one day. He said he wanted to marry me and that he could not live without me. Manasa said that Mahesh was good. He worked in a bank. I had completed my postgraduation and was looking for a job as a lecturer in a college. Manasa's husband, too, spoke to me, saying that Mahesh was very reliable; that he was not saying he loved me as a pretext for dating me, but that he wanted to marry me. I said Mahesh could talk to my father.

I laid down the condition that he should not object to my working after marriage. My parents fixed the wedding for only four months later. During those four months, the two of us went out several times. I noticed that Mahesh stared at good-looking and especially fair women in hotels and at bus stops and functions. I felt embarrassed and felt like questioning him. He would point at some random girl, praise her beauty and say, 'How could I be called a romantic person if I didn't look at the sunrise and beautiful girls?' I didn't like it at all. By then, the wedding cards had been printed and distributed.

It was one week before the wedding that Mahesh met me on the terrace at home. Resting his head in my lap, he said, 'Do you know Tapasvini, I went to the marriage of my cousin, Savitha, the other day. I saw a fair girl wearing a silk skirt. Do you know how beautiful she was! Throughout we were exchanging glances. I wanted to ask her name. But meanwhile someone called her Chanduri. She ran off. As she was going, she smiled at me naughtily, you know?' I was dumbstruck. I tried to push his head away from my lap but he got up and said, 'Shall I call you Chandu?' and kissed my lips deeply. I was frozen. He was intermittently calling me Chandu and locking lips. I pushed him away and despised him. It was my first kiss. He committed emotional adultery with some girl at a wedding and got stimulated. He recollected her and called me her name, kissed me and fulfilled his desire. How mean and hateful! How he had insulted and humiliated my body and my self-respect! I pushed him away and ran down the staircase. My body trembled with hatred. Mahesh shamelessly remarked, 'You are blushing too much.'

I rushed into my room, closed the doors and collapsed in my bed. My heart was breaking with rage. Che, I had goosebumps. I felt my lips. His saliva, che. He was thinking of someone else and dirtied my lips. I wished my lips would split, bleed and be purified! I washed my lips with water. That dirt wasn't going, despite repeated cleaning. I was blazing with grief. I cleaned my lips with soap and wiped them with a cloth. That dirt wasn't going. The kiss that was accompanied by his calling me Chandu polluted my body. What to do? How to bear that dirt? No, I could not live with that fellow. I should tell my parents that I don't want this marriage.

As soon as I opened the door, my maternal and paternal aunts and uncles, and grandmothers surrounded me, saying that my face was beaming with happy anticipation of the marriage. I couldn't say a word. My mother, father and sister were glowing with joy. 'I am sending three lakh rupees for the wedding. Don't worry, Nanna,' my brother was telling my father. Jalaja auntie said, 'Here is the long chain; the bangles, earrings and rings have also come.' The entire house was in a celebratory mood. All my energy waned. All this happiness would evaporate if I said I wouldn't marry Mahesh. Would my younger sister get married? She was doing her postgraduation at Osmania University. What to do? Just four days before the marriage!

My mind went blank. I stayed in my room, stopped eating and cried. People thought I was worried about leaving my parental home. My mother cried, fed me and pleaded with me, saying, 'Mahesh is a good man, my dear. You will be happy. Don't worry.' My innocent mother didn't know why I was crying. Did good mean just being six feet tall and fair, having a bank job, and owning a house and a car? How would they know about the dark corner in Mahesh that I knew of? They were already planning to get my sister married after my marriage. My head was splitting. I took a tablet and slept.

I was worried about my nuptial night and my marital life with him. I got the sacred thread tied by him like a scapegoat. I heaved a sigh when I heard that the nuptial night had been fixed after three days. I couldn't bear him being too close to my sister. Yamuna was fairer than me. He tried to talk to her even when there was no need to, looked at her closely and stared at her greedily every time he saw her, as if he would not be seeing her again. I hated it. One day, he caressed my cheeks, saying, 'Why don't you find out why your sister's cheeks are that fair and smooth?' I screamed at him, 'What are you talking about, Mahesh? Do you have any sense at all?'

Suddenly I remembered my sister's words before my marriage, 'Akka, bava came to my university twice on some work. He met me and took me to the canteen. My friends also came with us.' I was surprised and had asked Mahesh about it. He said carelessly, 'Yeah, I had gone as a student wanted an education loan. I met your sister as she was in the same university.' Surprised, I had asked him, 'The student would go to the bank if he required a loan. Why did you go?' He had quickly changed the topic, 'Agreed that you are very clever, stop your questions now, Tapasvi. I came all the way for you.' I remembered that conversation and said sternly, 'Don't talk to me about my sister again.' I went into my mother's room and cried, lamenting the misfortune of having to live with that fellow. Fair women were aphrodisiac for him.

I don't know how the nuptial night passed. I had entered the room with a million doubts. I refused to get decked up, but mother made me wear a white sari and jasmine flowers. I had goosebumps when he touched me. I pushed him away, saying, 'I need time. I am not psychologically ready.' But he forcibly entered me, saying, 'But I can't wait. I'm prepared.' He kissed me repeatedly, calling out, 'Yamuna, Yamuna.' I pushed him in shock. Mahesh was drunk. He did not listen to me. He completely violated me that night and crushed my youthful desires. I couldn't look into my sister's eyes the next day.

From then on, sex with him turned into a distressful experience and his kiss into a curse. He pushed his face against mine and forcibly and angrily turned my face towards himself when I protested and turned away. My lips, forehead, eyebrows, eyes and whole face hurt terribly. His mouth had the stink of the female names that he called out when he kissed me. Can what he did be called a kiss? Forcibly pushing his tongue into my mouth and salivating... I couldn't restrain myself from throwing up, nor did I have the energy to push him away. It was hell. In that hell, I gave birth to twins. Was compromise with this despicable man the only option that was left for me!

If ever I questioned him about his hungry gaze at women, he attributed it to his romantic nature. Sometimes he asked me in turn if it was wrong to look at women. He would giggle, saying, 'Do I look at every woman? I stare only at women who are fair and beautiful. I feel thrilled. Didn't I tell

you that I am an admirer of beauty?' Thrill, he said! Didn't I
know that it did not happen in his heart but between his legs!
Wasn't his calling the names of women a result of that thrill!
He accused me of becoming increasingly suspicious and a
suspicious demon. He told my friends, Manasa's husband and
my mother that I suspected him. He labelled me a suspecting
woman in front of everyone. I couldn't bear his gaze at other
women. That gaze led to kisses forced on me meant for
someone else followed by sexual assault on me.

If ever he looked hungrily at someone in the bus or
at some function, that someone was surely going to enter
my bedroom that night. That's why I hated and feared his
gaze. I hated my bedroom. Except me, my sister Yamuna,
Chandu, Nalini, Suneetha, Radha, Rajeswari, Jamuna,
Umadevi, Vijaya, Durga, and film actresses from Jayalalitha
to Nagma all stayed there. He described their bodies overtly
and remembered them while having sex with me. That is, he
was committing adultery. In a sense, I too was. Why should I
accept all this? For whom? For the children? What invisible
restrictions prevented me from escaping? I was a working
woman. Why was I surrendering to him? The children were
the sole reason. But for them, I would have escaped from
this mire long ago. The more I questioned him, the worse
he became. He turned violent. Before having sex, he wanted
me to recite the names of my sister, aunt, my friend and film
actresses. If I refused and tried to move away, he bashed me,
pulling me by the hair. Unable to bear the beatings, I even
recited a couple of names. He burnt me with a cigarette if

I refused. He felt provoked if I recited the names. Several times, I went to my parents' house and refused to come back. He came pleading and promising not to repeat what he had been doing. My mother advised me to make adjustments and mould myself according to his wishes. How could I explain to my mother that it was not just like wearing a sari of his choice? She said I shouldn't be suspecting my husband too much. I slipped into depression. I went to a psychiatrist when I couldn't manage the stress. I am taking medicines. I am able to live because of my children. I am able to teach in the class.

I asked the doctor if there were any medicines to reduce the unnatural sexual tendencies of my husband. The doctor, despite knowing about the depths of the wound in my heart, said casually, 'What's the big deal? This is very common in men. There is no thrill in sex without fantasy. Please cooperate with him. What's wrong with trying to get along with him?' Did this fellow too insult his wife in the same manner?

Fear of fair women! I had to stop the maid as he was stealing looks at her fair skin. Vajramma said that he had forcibly given her two hundred rupees. He had looked at her awkwardly. She had said she was not that kind and stopped coming to work. I was scared if the new tenants in the neighbourhood were fair. I heaved a sigh of relief if they were dark or wheatish. My condition was miserable. Once, Mahesh's boss invited us to his house for tea. He sat with his boss outside and I was with the women inside. After reaching home, the wretch asked me why they didn't let him sit with the women and if they were beautiful or not. He said,

'Though I was sitting with that fellow, my heart was dying to see the women inside.' I could feel my face going pale.

Another time, the son-in-law of the houseowners had passed away. We had recently shifted into that house. The women had unveiled their faces when they came to see the dead man. They looked like the stars peeping through the dark clouds. The grieving men stood at the gate to thank the visitors. This fellow was standing with them and looking at the women closely. When I went out to look for him, this is what I saw. He was shocked to see me. He almost dragged me home and shouted, 'Why are you here among the men!" He did not even consider that a death had taken place and that people were grieving over the loss. How shameless he was to use such an opportunity! What kind of a person was he!

I used to like the song *Mere saamne wali khidki mein ek chand ka tukda reheta hai* (a bit of the moon resides in the window across mine). Kishore Kumar's lovely song. Mahesh tried to sing this song, saying, 'Do you know, our neighbour Ravi's wife stands at the threshold for me when I go to office and when I return from office. Do you know how beautiful she is? Like the moon!' Not just that. He hummed the song when he returned home, with a glowing face. It was my favourite song, but I can't bear to hear that song now. When I screamed at him to stop singing the song, he accused me of being jealous. 'She is not even twenty years old. Look at her husband – he resembles a bear. Poor thing, don't know how she is able to take it,' he sighed. He stared at women, decided their age by calling them young and rejoiced proudly. Had I asked him about their age? What was this disease called?

How many wounds and how much violence everyday! Fear and hatred of having to live with Mahesh, of his kisses and of having sex with him. I wish I didn't have children. God, why did you give eyes to this fellow? I repeatedly wished he would lose his eyesight.

Mahesh would look at nude pictures of women on his phone. The display picture on his mobile was that of a half-nude film actress. He did not listen to me if I asked him to delete such pictures. If ever the children received his calls, they hated seeing those pictures. But Mahesh was shameless. I thought of teaching him a lesson. What if I called out the names of other men when he kissed me? Once, I put nude photos of male models in my notebook and left the notebook for him to see. He saw it and slapped me hard. He tore the photographs into pieces and stamped on them. He screamed, 'Are you acting like a courtesan?' and kicked me in the ribs. I almost fainted with pain, holding my ribs. I shouted, 'Why isn't it wrong if you see photographs?' I pounced on him and slapped him, shouting, 'I too feel like you. I too have anger and hatred like you.' I snatched the mobile phone from his hand and banged it on the floor. Mahesh got furious. What was my lean, weak body before his beastly strength! He did not change. I have a wish – a woman at whom Mahesh stared hungrily should beat him with her slipper in front of everyone, especially me.

He was the one who killed all my romantic longings with the very first kiss and made me feel frigid. My head became heavy as the past came alive in front of my eyes. Tears flowed down. It was five in the morning. I had to get up, become normal, cook and be smiling in front of my children, Ritvika and Kritika. They would ask endless questions if I looked worried.

Why did I have that dream? Did I think anything wrong when I was awake? No. I never met my childhood friend, Saranga, again.

Am I subconsciously waiting for a pure touch and kiss? With the person thinking only of me and chanting only my name? A kiss by a man with a passionate love for me…Yes, my lips are longing for such a kiss. How would it be if I kissed the person with equal passion? In my experience, a kiss is lips, forehead, eyebrows, eyes, cheeks and the entire face shrinking in excruciating pain and humiliation…Have I not been resisting such a kiss in the past six years and longing for a pure kiss? Am I searching for the lips that will kiss me with passionate love? Is it wrong? Recently, I read a Russian poet's poem in translation. How nice it was! The poetess Merina Tsvetaeva wrote on a kiss:

A kiss on the forehead!!!
The kiss on the forehead drives away distress
Let me kiss your forehead!
The kiss on the eyes lulls one to sleep
Let me kiss your eyes!
The kiss on the lips is like thirst-quenching water
Let me kiss your lips!
The kiss on the forehead wipes out sad memories

179

My dear…let me kiss your forehead again…!
Such great lines! Yes, I want such a kiss.

The kiss that I longed for, on my forehead, eyes, lips, every inch of my body, to drive away my sorrow, wipe out my sad memories, lull me to sleep like a baby and quench my thirst…the kiss that I have securely held! It is not possible with Mahesh.

Acknowledgements

I felt a compelling need to share my reading of Githanjali and my discovery of a feminist material with readers in English. I look upon my translation of Githanjali's stories into English as my intervention in the field of women's/feminist/sexuality studies. I must acknowledge the enthusiasm with which Githanjali discussed her writings with me. Thank you Githanjaligaru, for allowing me to enter and explore the world of your writings as a translator. Our long telephonic conversations have proved as inspiring as your writings have been for me. Thanks also to my friends and colleagues Professor Alladi Uma and Professor Sridhar for their meticulous reading of my translations and their feedback. I must especially thank Dr Shilpaa Anand who patiently listened to my narration of Githanjali's stories during our weekly voyage to a distant workplace. Probably that was my first translation of these stories. I owe thanks to my daughters Deepthi and Vennela for their continued support.

Thanks to everyone who contributed to this volume in myriad ways.

K. Suneetha Rani

Here I Am and other stories

by P. SATHYAVATHI

Translated from Telugu

'Sathyavathi's stories are powerful, deeply sensitive and widely varied in their themes, most of her writings concern women – women's lives and living, their dreams and disappointments, their losses and achievements.

'There is a constant search of truth in the present moment in her stories. Sathyavathi is anxious but not pessimistic, and uses a variety of techniques, sometimes satire, sometimes allegory, apart from direct storytelling, to aspire for a better world.

'Sathyavathi's powerful pen deserves serious recognition in India and abroad.'

NABANEETA DEV SEN, *Writer and academic*

'Sathyavathi's stories depict the social and psychological oppression of Indian women and reveal the hidden agenda of patriarchy to force women to submit themselves to its ideology...ignoring issues of their freedom, health and choice. Sathyavathi's stories diagnose the symptoms of this incurable disease. She observes and empathizes with the struggles and complexities of the less privileged just as a close friend would.'

M.M. VINODINI, *Writer, critic, activist and academic*

Echoes of the Veena and other stories
by R. Chudamani
Translated from Tamil by Prabha Sridevan

'R. Chudamani's style of writing is not loud and proclamatory. Her stories are about sensitive people, especially women, struggling in unspoken ways or with minimal ways of revealing their inner selves, to retain their sensitivity in today's world of gender violence, caste discrimination and elite arrogance.

'The stories in this collection like all her stories, are capable of touching the life of many. Stories are supposed to do that. It is not possible for all but that Chudamani is able to do it with her stories is a magic of her own that she has mastered.'

AMBAI, *Writer*

'The stories are marked by a sense of melancholy and rarely having a happy ending…Chudamani has a very simple yet hard-hitting language in her work. The stories are told from the perspective of the characters themselves, incorporating their feelings and prejudices, blaming no one but absolving no one, either.'

P.S. NISSIM, *The New Indian Express*

If A River and other stories
by KULA SAIKIA
Translated from Assamese

'These stories reveal the evolution of a brilliant writer who unravels the mysteries of life by reconstructing it, in a skilfully realistic way, which is unsettling, intriguing and delighting at once.'

K.R. MEERA, *Writer*

'Translated from Assamese, each of the 20 tales is narrated with a certain measure of delicacy and literary elegance…These come through a host of characters who seem to be seeking small pleasures in most mundane of situations, locations, relationships and social interactions but with significant profundity.'

SUPARNA-SARASWATI PURI, *The Tribune*

'The author uses characters to create his own world with delicate sensitivity depicting Assamese life in a subtle way by encompassing solitude, loneliness, alienation, strife, violence and beautiful nature.

'The author has succeeded in bringing out complexities of life in the remote North-Eastern part through his sensitive narration with precision.'

PRAKASH BAL JOSHI, *Free Press Journal*

RATNA TRANSLATION SERIES

After Yesterday and other stories
by APPADURAI MUTTULINGAM

Translated from Tamil by Padma Narayanan

'Tales of Lankan Tamil diaspora narrated with poignancy and hilarity.'

SREEVALSAN T., *Outlook*

'Appadurai Muttulingam's hilarious and at times thought-provoking tales about the lives of refugees living in nations across the globe make for interesting reading.

'Sparkling humour, unforgettable memories, gripping experiences, vivid descriptions, witty repartee and unexpected twists are just a few ingredients of this collection of refugee and fantasy-based futuristic tales . . . The book deserves a four star rating.'

N. JAGADESHWARI, *The Book Review*

'The stories in this collection are seemingly simple and just when you think you've figured them out, they spring a surprise on you.'

KRUPA GE, *Firstpost*

Some other titles from the
RATNA TRANSLATION SERIES

Here I Am and other stories by P. SATHYAVATHI
Translated from Telugu

Echoes of the Veena and other stories by R. CHUDAMANI
Translated from Tamil by Prabha Sridevan

If A River and other stories by KULA SAIKIA
Translated from Assamese

After Yesterday and other stories
by APPADURAI MUTTULINGAM
Translated from Tamil by Padma Narayanan

On A River's Bank by A. MADHAVAN
Translated from Tamil by M. Vijayalakshmi

A Faceless Evening and other stories
by GANGADHAR GADGIL
Translated from Marathi by Keerti Ramachandra

The Sixth Finger
by MALAYATOOR RAMAKRISHNAN
Translated from Malayalam by Prema Jayakumar

Havan by MALLIKARJUN HIREMATH
Translated from Kannada by S. Mohanraj

www.ratnabooks.in